I0628527

THE ISLAND OF CAPTAIN SPARROW

Borgo Press Books by S. FOWLER WRIGHT

*Arresting Delia: An Inspector Cleveland Classic Crime Novel * The Attic Murder: An Inspector Combridge & Mr. Jellipot Classic Crime Novel * The Bell Street Murders: An Inspector Combridge & Mr. Jellipot Classic Crime Novel * Beyond the Rim: A Lost Race Fantasy * Black Widow: A Classic Crime Novel * The Blue Room: A Novel of an Alternate Future * The British Colonies: No Surrender to Nazi Germany! * The Capone Caper: Mr. Jellipot vs. the King of Crime: A Classic Crime Novel * Crime & Co.: An Inspector Cleveland Classic Crime Novel * Dawn: A Novel of Global Warming * Dead by Saturday: An Inspector Cleveland Classic Crime Novel * Dream; or, The Simian Maid: A Fantasy of Prehistory (Marguerite Cranleigh #1) * Elfwin: An Historical Novel of Anglo-Saxon Times * The End of the Mildew Gang: An Inspector Cauldron Classic Crime Novel (Mildew #3) * Four Callers in Razor Street: An Inspector Combridge & Mr. Jellipot Classic Crime Novel * Four Days' War: The Alternate World War II, Book Two * The Hanging of Constance Hillier: An Inspector Cleveland Classic Crime Novel * The Hidden Tribe: A Lost Race Fantasy * Inquisitive Angel: A Novel of Fantasy * The Island of Captain Sparrow: A Lost Race Fantasy * The Jordans Murder: An Inspector Combridge & Mr. Jellipot Classic Crime Novel * The King Against Anne Bickerton: A Classic Crime Novel * Megiddo's Ridge: The Alternate World War II, Book Three * The Mildew Gang: An Inspector Cauldron Classic Crime Novel (Mildew #1) * Murder in Bethnal Square: An Inspector Combridge & Mr. Jellipot Classic Crime Novel * The Police and the Public: Some Thoughts on the British System of Justice * Post-Mortem Evidence: An Inspector Combridge & Mr. Jellipot Classic Crime Novel * Power: A Political Fantasy * Prelude in Prague: The Alternate World War II, Book One * Red Ike: A Novel of Cumberland (with J. M. Denwood) * The Return of the Mildew Gang: An Inspector Cauldron Classic Crime Novel (Mildew #2) * The Rissole Mystery: An Inspector Combridge & Mr. Jellipot Classic Crime Novel * The Screaming Lake: A Lost Race Fantasy * The Secret of the Screen: An Inspector Combridge & Mr. Jellipot Classic Crime Novel * The Song of Songs and Other Poems * Spiders' War: A Novel of the Far Future (Marguerite Cranleigh #3) * Three Witnesses: A Classic Crime Novel * Too Much for Mr. Jellipot: An Inspector Combridge & Mr. Jellipot Classic Crime Novel * The Vengeance of Gwa: A Fantasy of Prehistory (Marguerite Cranleigh #2) * Was Murder Done? A Classic Crime Novel * Who Murdered Reynard? A Classic Crime Novel * The Wills of Jane Kanwhistle: An Inspector Combridge & Mr. Jellipot Classic Crime Novel * With Cause Enough?: An Inspector Combridge & Mr. Jellipot Classic Crime Novel * The World Below: A Science Fiction Novel * Wyndham Smith: His Adventures in the 45th Century: A Science Fiction Novel*

THE ISLAND OF CAPTAIN SPARROW

A Lost Race Fantasy

by

S. FOWLER WRIGHT

THE BORGO PRESS

An Imprint of Wildside Press LLC

MMX

Copyright © 1928 by S. Fowler Wright
Copyright © 2010 by the Estate of S. Fowler Wright

All rights reserved.
No part of this book may be reproduced in any form
without the expressed written consent
of the author and publisher.

www.wildsidebooks.com

FIRST WILDSIDE EDITION

CONTENTS

CHAPTER ONE

THE LANDING OF CHARLTON FOYLE

The wind had fallen, but the sky was still black with low and hurrying cloud, and the sea rolled heavily.

Charlton Foyle sat in the stern of the boat, and steered with an oar. He was striving to keep her head before the wind, and gazing anxiously at the land, towards which wind and tide were united to take him.

He saw that the cliff wall rose straight and high. There was no sign of nearer rocks or shallows. It appeared that the cliff rose abruptly from a deep water. What hope could it give?

He could not handle the boat. There was a mast, but it was not stepped, nor had he strength and skill to set it up, or to control its canvas. There were oars, but they were too heavy, and the boat too large for a single man to manage more than one.

Till the storm came in the night he had let the boat drift as it would. He had water, he had food. He had not known where he was, nor in which direction land might be nearest. His only hope was to be picked up by a passing ship, so he saved his strength and ate little.

For many days the sun shone, and the seas were kind. The indolent, laughing waters had rocked him gently, and in their arms he had regained something of the health which he had sought vainly over half the world. He had begun to care for life, when life seemed most likely to elude him. He was aware that he watched the horizons for lift of sail, or trail of smoke, with a keener vigilance than he had done in the weariness of the first days. But it was still with a mind too indifferent to the future for anxiety to disturb it, unless it were aroused by a danger which should be acute and imminent.

He had leaned lazily over the tossing side of the boat, watching strange life in deep water, or gazed at a sky of white and blue, brilliant with tropic stars.

Once a flock of birds passed, low and swift, over the waves. He did not know their kind. They flew straight and fast, as having a clear goal and a common purpose. Should he make some effort to direct the boat in the same way? Even could he do it, he had doubted its wisdom. He knew nothing of how far such birds may travel. They might be on their way to a near land, or they might be leaving the near land behind them. They passed quickly, and the great loneliness of sky and water was again around him.

Once the wide expanse of solitary sky was specked by a great bird that grew in size as it came more nearly overhead. He realised that it was not merely flying over, but was descending toward him. It was grey in colour, larger than a swan, and with broad wings that moved with an occasional powerful stroke. It came low. It circled the boat twice in a narrowing spiral. He saw a long, hooked beak, and a dark eye that considered him. He reached for a boat-hook, and was aware that his hand shook as he did so.

Then it came with a rush, close over him. He crouched in the well of the boat, and thrust blindly as it passed.

Because he crouched as he did, the beak missed him. For a second he was under a canopy of feathered wings. The boat-hook caught and came clear.

He saw the great bird soaring back into the sky. There was a stain of blood on the end of the hook, and some grey feathers floated on the wind, and settled down on the water.

When the wind had risen, he had got out the oar and striven to keep the boat's head so that she should not be swamped by the waves. He did not know whether his toil had been needless. The boat was large, strongly built, and half-decked. He supposed that the storm had not been a bad one. Certainly not as bad as some that he had witnessed from a liner's deck. But the waves had seemed large—there was a difference in the point of view.

Anyway, the wind had fallen again. The black menace of the night, with its heaving waters that came out of the darkness, was over, and he was safe, though wearied—and now the sea was carrying him swiftly toward a peril which he had no means of avoiding, or any hope to overcome . Every moment the cliff-wall showed nearer and higher as the tide swept the boat forward.

At the rate at which it was moving, it obeyed the steering-oar very readily. He could deflect its course, but he doubted whether this would avail him. It might enable him to delay the final impact, or to strike the land somewhat farther north than would otherwise be the case, but it seemed that, soon or late, he must be dashed against a cliff-wall that showed neither beach nor break so far as his eyes could follow it.

Still, the impulse is instinctive to delay a danger which we can see no means of defeating. The swimmer will remain afloat while his strength lasts, though he may have no hope of rescue. The embarrassed tradesman will strive to renew a bill, though, as he well knows, the later date will give no better prospect of solvency. He leant on the oar till the boat lay almost broadside to an advancing wave. It rolled in the trough, and some water slopped over the gunwale.

Easing it somewhat, he looked shoreward again as the next wave lifted. The morning sun, which was behind him, and still low in the sky, found a break in the flying cloud, and lighted the cliff-face with a fading glory. But he noticed that there was one spot which remained dark. It was not a break in the wall. It was like a cave-mouth at the tide-level. It gave a hope, though a faint one. He bent his mind to the task of steering toward it.

As he approached the cliff he saw that the distant view had not enlarged its terrors. It rose straight as a wall. If his boat were beaten against it by the breaking waves, he knew that disaster must be instant and irretrievable.

It seemed, as he neared it, that the pace of the boat was somewhat less, and that his control upon it increased. He wondered whether he might not be wiser to struggle to avoid the peril entirely. Soon or late, changes of wind and tide would be sure to aid him. But the chance was doubtful. His control of the boat, at the best, was not great. If he should work it some distance from the land, the next tide might fling it back, and there might then be no possibility of refuge.

Now, the opening which he had sought was before him, widening in appearance as he approached, and of such height that a fishing-smack could have run in with its sails set.

He was aided, more than he knew, by the fact that the tide was full, and near the turn; and, more by the tide's caprice than his own skill, he steered to the opening.

The waves that broke on the cliff-wall to right and left made a swirling turmoil of the gap which gave them passage. They rolled the boat till he thought that it would be overset, swept it broadside on, and carried it into a tunnel where it bumped heavily against a wall of rock, recoiled, and the next moment was in somewhat quieter water.

He perceived that the tunnel, though straight in itself, was driven into the cliff obliquely from the sea-line. The cliff faced the east. The tunnel ran north-west. The direct force of the waves did not therefore swing in; yet the boat tossed from side to side, and though he struggled hard with the oar, it got some rough bumps as the waves hurried it inward.

As his eyes became used to the gloom, he saw that the passage ended in a blank wall, against which the water rose and fell restlessly, making a murmurous sound which filled the tunnel. The speed of the boat slackened as he approached it. He shipped the oar and took up the boat-hook, thinking to fend the boat from the wall of rock which he was nearing. He saw no hope but to remain there and protect the boat as best he might, till the tide should carry him again to the open sea. Then he noticed a heavy iron ring, set in the face of the rock, by which a boat might be moored. He looked round with an increased wonder and a keener scrutiny. He saw that there were similar rings in the walls on either side. The tunnel had steadily narrowed as it progressed, so that the walls were much nearer than they had been at the entrance. It was evident that a boat moored to the three rings would be secure from being beaten against the rocks. He had abundance of stout cable, and he resolved to fasten it in this manner. He could at least feel that he would not be hurried out to the open sea, till he should be ready for the adventure.

Commencing to carry out this plan, which was not easy for one man only in the unquiet boat, he had to consider the length of free cable which he should allow. If it were much, the boat would not be centrally held; if little, how would it fare when the tide fell? And it could not fall with it, unless the cables broke. He pictured one breaking, while the others held, and the boat tipped up and its precious cargo scattered into the water.

It was true that he could watch, and pay out or shorten the cables as the need changed, but that could scarcely have been the intention of those who provided this means of security. He was led to wonder how deep might be the water beneath him. He sounded with the boat-hook, and struck rock at about four feet from the surface.

Reassured, he continued his work. If the tide, as he rightly supposed, were full, then his fears were groundless. Even while he worked he knew that this was so, and that the boat was pulling outward on the ropes that held it.

Also, as he worked, he observed another thing with a fresh wonder. In the inner corner a flight of steps rose in the rock. They were very roughly cut, mere holes for the toes to enter. At intervals at either side, staples were fixed for the climber's hands to grip. The ladder—if it could be held worthy of such a name—ended in a black hole in a corner of the rock roof.

Surely, he thought, if human hands had hollowed that great tunnel, they would have given it a less perilous exit. But the hands might not be the same—or they might not have intended that the ascent should be easy.

He considered whether he should attempt to explore it. He did not know what hostility he might arouse. He knew that the cargo which his boat contained would excite the cupidity of all but the most ignorant savages, and from such as they he might encounter a different danger. He believed that he was off the tracks of sea traffic, or of charted land, and he knew that the lonelier islands of the vast Pacific were the last homes of cannibalism, and of a savagery which appeared to be unable to understand any argument but that of extermination.

He realised that, should he climb those steps, his return could not be rapid, at whatever urgency. He realised also that, as the tide fell and his boat grounded, he would be trapped beyond the possibility of flight, should be continue to occupy the tunnel.

On the other hand, the sea offered a precarious hospitality. The steps that fronted him were the only possible alternative. Though it was true that his boat would become immobile as the water fell, it was equally so that no other boat could enter upon him at such a period.

The fact that there was provision for mooring a boat, and that it was vacant, suggested either that the tunnel was unused, or that those who occupied it were absent upon the sea.

He decided to wait till the tide fell, and, if nothing had then happened, he would climb the steps in the assurance that no one could approach the boat in his absence, or attack him in the rear of his exploration.

Meanwhile he was well armed, and none could come upon him hurriedly by such a descent. If a boat should enter while still the water allowed it, he would be trapped indeed, but that risk must be taken, and already it was almost over. There was a repeating rifle in the boat, and this he found and laid near to his hand while he manipulated the mooring ropes so that the boat was drawn close to the steps, and the hollow to which they led was directly above him.

He looked up, but he could see nothing. The hole was square and black.

So he sat there, watching the tossing sunlit water at the cave-mouth, and the black vacancy above him, the rifle across his knee. After a time the boat grounded, gently enough, and the water receded from it. He looked to see the whole passage draining equally, but the waves still swept in. He perceived that the floor, which was now bare around him, sloped downward toward the entrance.

As the water receded, he left the boat, and followed it, not being minded to pursue his first intention until he were satisfied that entrance from seaward would be difficult or impossible. He thought also that, if he could look outward from the tunnel, he could observe whether there was any sign of human life on the waters.

He found leisure as he waited to wonder that the floor of the tunnel was bare and black as the waves left it. He would have thought that such a cave would be a trap for sand and shell and all the ocean's debris. But he supposed that the smooth slope caused it to be washed clear as the tide receded.

Having no haste, he did not attempt to wade ahead of the tide's retreat. It was a fortunate leisure, as he had realised before he stood, at a later hour, looking over an ocean which sparkled to a tropic sun and showed no sail. For the gentle slope had ended abruptly halfway down the passage, leaving only a narrow ledge of rock to follow on the left hand, apart from which the rock fell across the whole width to a depth he could not tell, for, when the tide had fallen a dozen feet below, it had not found its limit.

But he was satisfied to see that, by this time, there was no way of gaining access from the empty seas except, it were, by the climbing of twelve feet of wall-like rock, against which the waves beat continually.

There were not even any steps such as those which he had resolved to attempt. He judged that they who made or used this tunnel, whether it were yesterday or a thousand years ago—and it might be either for any means he had of deciding—did not intend that it should be entered except at high tide, and that it was very certain that no one was now likely to attempt it.

He walked back confident that his rear was secure, and resolved to explore the mystery to which the steps led upward.

CHAPTER TWO

HOW HE CAME TO THE ISLAND

It was two months or more since Charlton Foyle had booked a passage to Honolulu on a trading schooner. He had been wandering aimlessly in the summer ways of the world, avoiding the death to which a dozen doctors had doomed him, yet not gaining the health without which life is of a doubtful value.

At Honolulu he had asked to continue on the schooner indefinitely. He did not like the two men who appeared to be the joint owners of the vessel, but that was an unimportant consideration, for he was indifferent to those around him. The schooner was well-found. He had lived less luxuriously on liners of fifty times the tonnage. He felt that the voyage had been beneficial beyond his previous experiences, and was anxious to continue it. They had demurred at first. They excused themselves on the plea that they would be visiting a succession of distant islands, at some of which they might be detained, and that the date of their return was uncertain. When they found that this did not deter him, they named a figure which they probably thought would be prohibitive. But in the end they had agreed, though with obvious reluctance, and after a quarrel between themselves, which he had partly overheard, though he did not understand its meaning. In view of what he knew later, he was surprised that they had consented at all—unless they were each so afraid of the treachery of the other that they welcomed even a stranger, who must be an embarrassment later. Unless, of course, he were—removed.

He did not know, even now, what dark secrets might explain the events which had followed—which do not concern us now—though it is a tale which might be worth the telling. He only knew that, after a load, of whatever nature, had been taken aboard in the night-time from a nameless beach, they had burst into a sudden quarrel in which knives had been drawn, and from which they had been separated by the efforts of a crew which appeared to consist about equally of the adherents of either.

And then, on a later night, when he had lain on deck, as he sometimes did, unsuspected in the shadows, and they were anchored beside another nameless beach, a boat had been lowered and stealthily loaded by the men who held the watch, one of the partners superintending. And just as it appeared that the work was finished, the other had rushed up, with his party behind him, and the deck had become the scene of sudden violence, oaths, bare knives, and pistol-shots, and the cough of a dying man.

On a moment's impulse he had dropped over the side into the loaded boat, as the nearest safety from the flying shots of a quarrel which did not concern him, and then become aware, with mingled feelings, that the mooring-rope had parted, and that he was adrift on the ocean.

The distance had widened rapidly from the anchored schooner, while the noise of the fight continued and fell. After an interval of silence, he had heard two shots, and had supposed that the victorious party were disposing of what remained of their opponents. Then there had been a brief silence again, and then a pandemonium of cries that told that the loss of the boat had been discovered.

Should he hail them? He had experienced a natural hesitation. There would be so little difference in one shot more, and one more corpse for the sea's disposal. And, while he doubted, he drifted farther away, into a momentary security, for the night was dark and starless.

As he drifted thus, he realised that his peril might be the greater for his silence, were he to be in sight of the ship when the dawn rose, and that his alternative was to be an outcast in the loneliest wastes of the Pacific, where a thousand miles were unsailed and uncharted. But even while he realised his dilemma, the difficulty of explaining his silence had increased, and the distance widened. The ennui of his physical condition inclined him to the choice of inaction. The cries grew fainter and died away.

The dawn showed him an open ocean, without sail or sight of land.

CHAPTER THREE

THE INTERIOR OF THE CLIFF

It was typical of Charlton's disposition, though a condition of health rather than character, that, having assured himself that his rear was secure, and decided his purpose, he was in no haste to commence it. He became conscious that he was hungry, and ate a meal at his leisure. Having done this, he was increasingly aware that he was tired from a night's vigil, and from the toils in which he had spent it. As the time passed, and there came no threat from the dark aperture above him, he became assured that it held no menace. He did not resolve on sleep, rather it resolved upon him, as he ignored it idly. In the end, sleep he did, and for some hours, though his sleep was light and watchful.

Doubtless, when he awoke, he was the better for sleep and food, and went about his preparations with a careful deliberation. In the boat there was a lantern, which he lit, and, having no belt, he fastened it round him with a length of rope. He placed a loaded revolver in a right-hand pocket. He looked with hesitation at a very serviceable sword, straight and sharp, neither too light nor too heavy, which was among the boat's offensive equipment, but he rejected the thought. It was unlikely enough that he would meet with any living thing. If he should do so, they might not be unfriendly. If they were doubtful in their demeanour, a display of weapons would not increase their goodwill. More definite in its objection was the fact that he was not used to the wearing of such a weapon, and that it might impede his legs in climbing. Every way the revolver was best and should be sufficient.

The climb was not easy. The supports, through firm enough, of whatever age or metal, seemed very far apart. The foot-holes were sometimes difficult to find. Clinging closely to the face of the rock, he had to grope for them with a free foot, the hold of the other sometimes feeling insecure as he did so. He wondered whether the staples would hold, were his whole weight suddenly dragged upon them. He did not like the thought of falling upon the hard stone below. He imagined himself there with a broken leg, struggling to get into the boat before the returning water should drown him and his life afterwards, if he should be able to live under such conditions. The penalties of accident are heavy to a lonely man.

His arms ached badly. Probably he threw more strain upon them than a more accustomed climber would have done, and his muscles were unused to such effort.

When it seemed that he could climb no more, he realised that it might be harder to return than to continue. He rested for a few moments, so far as rest was possible in such a posture, and started upward again. A doctor might have told him that such experiences were all that was needed to complete a cure that the sea-winds had made possible. A man may die in a gradual lethargy, thinking that he has no will to live, who would yet be roused by a sudden threat of death, before he had gone too low for his will to wake to the conflict.

He was impeded also by the lantern, which would not keep clear of the wall, as he had designed to sling it, but he was glad of its light when he came at last to a place of landing.

At least—should he land? For some time he had left behind the open space of the tunnel and had been ascending a narrow shaft about a yard square. It still continued upward into the darkness, but behind him there was now an opening into an unlighted chamber. Loosing one hand, he leaned sideways from the wall and raised the lantern. He saw nothing but a bare rock floor and an empty darkness. He was aching to rest his straining arms, and for the security of a solid floor, but still he hesitated. He did not doubt that he could step safely to the floor that was about three feet behind him—but the return? He thought that it might not be so easy to reach forward and clutch the rings, or to stride over vacancy to those precarious foot-holds. He had a vision of starving there with all his stores beneath him. The bare darkness of the chamber gave no promise of hospitality, nor probability of exit. It might be that the way out (if way there were) was to continue upward.

While he doubted, weariness solved the problem. He was too exhausted for descent or for further climbing. He reached out a foot, felt firm rock, leaned his weight upon it, and landed easily.

After a short rest, he commenced to explore the chamber. He was not keenly curious, nor did he feel anxious as to what he might discover. The physical exhaustion following the exertions of the night and day acted on a body which was still searching for health rather than having found it, and left his mind dull and aloof from his surroundings, now that the need for further effort had lost its urgency.

The lantern showed him a rock chamber, bare and black, about ten feet high, and of about twice that width. Its length was greater, and the light was insufficient to reveal it fully. He judged that its direction was towards the cliff-face, which limited its possibility.

He decided to make a circuit of the walls. If they should show no exit, he must continue to climb into the darkness or give up the enterprise and return to such hospitality as the sea might offer.

Turning to the short inner wall, he came at once to an open passage about three feet broad, and high enough for a man to walk freely. This must run inland, he thought, and gave a better prospect of reaching the surface. So far as the light showed, it was not level, but sloped steadily, though not steeply, upward.

He took a few steps along it and then returned, reluctant to leave an unexplored possibility of danger behind him. He would not risk the chance of anyone cutting off his return to the boat or gaining possession of it in his absence. He resolved that he would first complete the circuit of the walls of the chamber.

Emerging from the passage again, he took the wall left-hand, casting the light before him. He trod in a fine dry dust, which increased in depth as he went forward. The light flickered upon the length of the northern wall. Dim and huge, he caught the figure of a man. He stopped, lifting the light to look more closely. He saw the drawing of a human form, with wide, stag-like horns. It was coloured a dull red. The figure was crude, powerful, brutal. It was human, and yet not human. It might be god—or devil. It might be the work of an artist to whom the two had been one. Because art cannot be powerful without sincerity, no artist of our own or of any historic period could have drawn that figure. Charlton may not have realised this, but he recognised that he was looking upon the work of a dim antiquity.

The figure was not more than eight feet high, including the horns, yet it gave an impression of overshadowing size, and of an insatiable ferocity. He shivered, as though chilled, though the cavern was not cold.

He noticed that the figure held a sword in its left hand. He thought that its shape was not unlike that which he had left in the boat. He had an absurd fancy that it was the same. Always the sword, he thought. Races and civilisations rise and die, and their records pass from the minds of men, but the sword continues. Always the sword. His mind wondered and wandered. The figure held it hypnotised. He pulled himself free with difficulty. He looked down in the dust in which he trod—a very fine dry dust—and it had a new significance. It was the dust of things long dead—very long dead.

He went on with altered feelings, as of one who invaded an ancient sanctuary, or a forgotten tomb. The thought that he must beware of the presence of living men had left him wholly. And then, as he completed the length of the chamber—it was surprisingly long— and turned the corner to the shorter wall, he came on something which obliged him to adjust his mind afresh. It was a brass cannon. He saw it while still a few feet away, and at the first glance it was unmistakable. Coming closer, he saw that it was swivel-mounted, of no recent pattern. He ran the light along it, touching it in wonder to assure himself of its reality. It was covered with a thin coating of dust. He noticed a hint of verdigris at the touch-hole. Otherwise it showed clear and bright as he rubbed the dust aside. He thought that he saw some writing upon it—or was it ornamental scrollwork only? Looking more closely, he read—*The Fighting Sue*, 1866. That was definite; but it might have been at a later date that it found its home in this solitude. He looked round for anything which might give further explanation, but he found nothing. There was no powder or ball. There was no other object.

A line of light, very faint, which did not come from the lantern, caught his notice. Looking at the wall which fronted the cannon's muzzle, he saw a wooden shutter, wide and low, beneath which the light entered. It was made of a hard, elm-like wood, showing no sign of decay. It was suspended on a long horizontal hinge. He tried to raise it, and found that he could do so after some effort, though it did not move easily. He looked through an embrasure cut through two feet of rock. It was not very large on its inner side, but it was shaped in a widening funnel, sloping downward. It showed a broad extent of ocean below him, with long waves rolling inward. If it had been made for the cannon, it, at least, must be recent. But what purpose of defence could it serve—could it ever have served—in this lonely place? Who had left it, and how, and when?

He could find no answer.

But he saw that there were traces of two occupations: one of an incalculable antiquity, and one which, in comparison, was but of yesterday.

With this thought in mind, he observed that the dust was much thicker along the walls than in the centre of the chamber, where it had the impression of many feet, and, looking closely, he was sure that some at least of these feet had been booted.

He completed the examination of the remaining wall, but made no further discovery.

He paused again at the mouth of the shaft, hesitating as to whether he should return to the boat, or explore the tunnel before doing so. He could not resolve the significance of all that he had seen, but it had diminished both his hope and his fear. He now imagined himself alone in a place where man had once been, but which they had long deserted. He had no reason to fear any hostility, nor to hope for any assistance.

On the whole he was relieved. He was in no urgent need of the necessities of life, at the lack of which a man must look round for the help of his fellows. He had much to excite cupidity. Should he meet with men here, it was little likely that they would be of his race or language, or of a natural friendliness.

The one problem which remained was that of an inland exit from the passage which he had discovered. That was, at least, probable.

If there were none, his course was clear. He must put to sea again when the conditions appeared favourable. His water would not last forever. That consideration alone was decisive, for these caves showed no stream, nor any faintest trickle of moisture. If he put to sea again, he might find another side to the land where it would be possible to beach the boat without danger. But this was doubly doubtful, for he knew that his measure of control of the boat gave little prospect of reaching such a goal, did it exist, of which he had no evidence.

On the other hand, if he should find that the passage gave him access to a desert land, he would have to decide whether it would be better to remain there or to risk the dangers of the sea once more, after he had replenished his stock of water and perhaps augmented the store of food which he carried. It was no hopeful prospect to drift at the mercy of sea and wind, knowing that his life was forfeit to the first serious storm that the days would bring. But then there would be no haste to decide. Really, there was no haste now. He felt tired and lethargic. Had the return to the boat been easier, he would have taken it at once, and rested there before he explored further.

As it was, he stood hesitating, and the lantern decided him. The light flickered, and he observed that the candle which it contained was almost finished. The thought that he might be obliged to stride across the hollow shaft in the darkness woke a sudden panic. Very carefully, lest a jerk should extinguish it, he slung the lantern to his side. He saw the metal loops in the wall before him, and in the urgency of the failing light he leaned forward boldly to grasp them. He hung a moment while his feet scraped for the holes, and the light went out as he found them. But it was easier to descend than it had been to climb upward, and he had beneath him a more definite and desired objective.

It was long after noon when he regained the boat, and the tide had risen far, though it had not yet reached it. He had gained this much by his enterprise, that he was no longer anxious lest any hostility should threaten him from the aperture above him. If there were any men living who had access to that gloomy chamber (which he greatly doubted), they were making no use of their knowledge, and it was little likely that they would be aware of his presence. He ate with an appetite such as he had not known for a long time; after which, he decided to wait till the next day before continuing his exploration. He put a fresh candle into the lantern, though he did not light it, laid it beside the loaded rifle, near to his hand, and settled himself into the bed which he had made in the stern of the boat, on which he had slept so many nights while the summer seas had rocked him.

He did not sleep at once, as he had expected to do. He lay awake till the darkness came, and the boat was lifted again in the arms of the advancing water. He felt her pull on the cables, now on this, now on that, as the waves swayed her. Soon she settled to a motion which was gentler and more regular than that to which he had been accustomed on the open sea. But still he did not lose consciousness. Perhaps he missed the stars overhead. When at last he slept, he dreamed—dreams of the kind which cause the sleeper to wake with a sense of misery and foreboding beyond reason.

He dreamed that he was in the water, struggling toward a distant shore. In fact, he could not swim, nor could he have told from recollection of his dreams with what stroke he contrived it. A dream will avoid difficulties of that kind, leaving some things in vague outline, while others are of a very vivid distinctness. He had a long knife in his hand. He could see the shore as he swam: a slope of sand, with a dark green line of trees beyond it. He was wondering whether he would reach it, or the sharks would get him. With the thought, he became aware of one which swam close under him, a moving shadow in a green depth of water. He saw it turn, and the toothed mouth open. He knew that the next second it would come with a rush to seize him in that fatal vice. He dived sideways and saw the white belly shoot past him. As it did so, he struck into it with the knife he held. He kept his grip on the haft, and was dragged rapidly through the water. It. cut a long slit in the shark's belly, with a sound like the tearing of cloth. It was not that he cut it: the great fish cut itself open by the speed of its rush. He simply held on to the knife and was dragged along with it. The water round him was red, and the shark was gone. He swam on. He was on the sandy beach, walking towards the shelter of the trees beyond it. The sun was high. The sand burned his naked feet. He looked toward the welcome shade ahead, and suddenly his mind changed and he was afraid. It was a jungle toward which he was walking, dense, black, silent, and menacing. He did not know what he feared, but he knew that he dared not enter it. He had no plan—no hope—the jungle terrified him. He watched its shadows in dread of what might emerge to destroy him...and the hot sand burnt his feet.

He woke to a dense blackness, very different from the open nights to which the last weeks had used him. In the tunnel the midnight darkness was absolute. It was full of the sound of waters that tossed and strained the boat which was his only safety, but he could see nothing. He could not have slept very long, or the tide would have receded again. A sense of loneliness oppressed him. He realised his isolation, as he had not done previously, even when adrift at night upon the solitude of the ocean. And the dream would not leave his mind. It was associated in some way which he could not understand with the deserted chamber above him, and that also had become an unearthly terror.

He was not naturally without fortitude, and he resisted the oppression which had invaded his mind, facing the dream squarely, and reasoning with himself upon it. It was an absurd dream, but not otherwise remarkable. Certainly, he could not kill sharks in the water. But he had watched them from the schooner's deck. One had followed his boat for several days. It was not unnatural that he should dream of it. It would have been natural enough that he should have dreamt of it with terror. But, in fact, he had not done so. Vivid though the moment had been when he had driven in the knife as the shark passed him, it had not frightened him in the dream. The recollection did not frighten him now. It was the darkness beneath the trees—there was some horror there. If he should enter, it would be worse than death...and there was no other way.

He faced it, but it would not yield to his reason. He tried to think of other things, but it would not be forgotten. In some way, the black secret of the jungle and the mystery of the chamber above him were one, and were united for his destruction. Had there been any light at all, he felt that he would have loosed the boat and drifted out with the tide. Yet the effort he made to resist this oppression of cowardice cannot have been without result, for in the end he slept again and wakened to find a dim light around him, and to see a shaft of morning sunlight striking the wall at the tunnel entrance.

CHAPTER FOUR

THE FOREST

He woke in a different mood from that with which the night had assailed him. He cared nothing for dreams, or for the dust of forgotten days. He was of no mind to venture again upon a deserted ocean in a boat which he could not guide, if there were any better possibility. By the coastline he had seen he judged that the land must be of considerable extent. If it were uninhabited, it might give the means of sustaining life very easily in such a latitude. The cave above him offered shelter already which appeared to be his for the taking. If there were other inhabitants, they might be friendly. He could explore with caution. He need not show himself till he were sure that it would be safe to do so. Everything depended upon a landward exit to the passage he had discovered, or to the shaft above, and surely it was probable that one of these would give it.

He became keen to start, hurrying his morning meal, and even considered carrying up some of his possessions, his mind beginning to regard the upper chamber as his headquarters, rather than the boat which had brought him to it. He resisted this impulse, but he started in good spirits, equipped for a day's absence. He was less indifferent to life, and more alert to meet it than he had been for years. Circumstance had pressed upon him till he had been forced to react against it, and it had occupied his mind so that he was not even aware of the change which it had induced.

He climbed more quickly than yesterday, and was soon in the deserted chamber. He resolved to examine it once again before entering the tunnel, lest he should have overlooked anything of significance on his first circuit.

He found nothing, but, coming to the wooden shutter which covered the embrasure, it occurred to him that he would gain some light if he should fasten it upwards. Examination showed that this had been done by means of short chains and staples which were fixed into the rock. Having raised it thus, and satisfied himself that it was firmly held, he leaned out to survey the scene beneath him. It was idly done, a moment's gazing at the sunlit water before he returned his eyes to the dark interior. He had little hope of any rescuing sail from that lonely ocean, and he had ceased to fear that any hostile craft might be seeking the place of his refuge. His mind was on other things, and when his eye fell upon the smoke of a steamer clear in view upon the horizon beneath him, there was a moment's delay before he realised its significance. Then his mind rapidly debated the possibility of signalling, either from where he stood, or by returning to the boat.

He could think of no method which would be hopeful and for which time would allow, unless the ship were approaching while he prepared it, and as he watched, he knew that that was not the case. Already it was disappearing below the curve of the world.

So he did nothing, and watched it go, but the incident gave him an impression that he was not outside the area of the peopled seas, and that the land on which he stood must be known and might be inhabited by those who were at least in touch with civilisation, and this conclusion may have given him a greater confidence in the initial stages of the adventure which was before him.

It was a natural conclusion, but a mistaken one. The ship he saw had been driven for three weeks with a broken propeller, at the mercy of the southeast trade winds. It was only a few days earlier that it had been repaired, and she was now heading due north for the Golden Gate, through seas which her captain had never known, though he had spent his life in the highways of the Pacific. He had been startled a few hours before by a cry of "Land ahead!" in an ocean which the charts gave as deep water, with the nearest island a thousand miles away. He was in the cabin with his second officer as

Charlton watched the disappearing vessel. He had an obsolete chart of a previous century spread out before him. It was vague and doubtful in its warnings, or entirely blank in many areas, and when it was definite, it was usually wrong, but at the spot over which they were then sailing an island of considerable area had been vaguely indicated. The authority for the existence of this island was in a note which the captain was reading:

"In 1744, Capt. Geo. Cooper, of the brig *Good Adventure*, reported that, having been driven many miles out of his course by storms and contrary winds, in which he had lost a mast and suffered other damage, and having been afterwards becalmed for seventeen days, a wind coming at length, he did shortly sight a large island, in lat. E. 123° 4'7" long. N. 5° 2'8", on which he would have landed, but that he found it to be surrounded on all sides by high and inaccessible cliffs, giving no hope of harbour. Being short of water and other furnishings, he did sail round it, but found no bay or inlet where he might anchor. Its circumference was about twenty miles, but he neither saw sign of life, nor did he believe that any could ever have landed upon it."

The two men looked at each other with the same thought in the minds of both. How could an island of such extent—from the circumference given, it might be anything from ten square miles to twenty-five—having been once discovered, have been lost and forgotten during the past two centuries?—and this in the equatorial region of the Northern Pacific? It was strange enough, but they did not think it so strange as a landsman might. They knew too much of the vast spaces over which they trafficked. It was not only that it lay remote from other lands—the Marquesas Islands were fifteen hundred miles to the southwest, the speck of Duncan Island was twelve hundred miles to eastward, Christmas Island was two thousand miles due west, and there was no nearer land—but that it lay apart from the ocean highways, and in that belt of tropic calms which the trade winds leave between them. It was a region which the sailing ships had dreaded, even when their routes were obliged to cross it, and which the steam-driven vessels of later days would take indifferently in the direct line of their purpose, and in that only. They knew that there are parts in the Pacific where the stream of traffic is as unceasing as in the main street of a busy town, and vast stretches were a ship might anchor till its crew should die of senility without sight of any other vessel to invade their solitude, and vast tracts also where, it may be, no sail has risen from the dawn of time.

An inaccessible island? It might well be. They had seen the abrupt unfriendly height of its southern shores, on which they would surely have perished had they not approached when there was daylight to warn them; they were now passing its eastern side, and the same prospect faced them. Anyway, he could do no more than report his discovery—or rather, that of the master of the *Good Adventure*, who had seen and told. He had beaten round its perilous cliffs in his two-masted brig as good seamanship contrived and winds permitted. No one had confirmed his tale, and, as the years passed, it had been discredited. Well, he would be justified in the end.

Captain Markham, a precise man, made his records in a neat, small hand. It might not be the only island of which the charts gave no warning. It was a case for soundings and more soundings. He would take no rest till he should be in better-known and safer seas. He went back to the bridge.

Meanwhile, Charlton Foyle, with a confidence curiously reinforced by that evidence of the passing nearness of his civilised kind, was going up the dark tunnel. It was a gentle, steady ascent, straight and long. The tunnel was quite dry. The air was good enough, though he could feel no current. Becoming curious on the point, he exposed the flame of the lantern. It bent, though very slightly. It indicated a very gentle passage of air in the direction in which he was going. He took this to imply that there must be some opening before him, and his pace increased, though he watched his steps carefully. After what he thought to be about half a mile, the ascent ceased. For a short distance the floor was level, then it began to descend. Here he passed an opening on his left hand, but he decided to continue straight forward. There was still no sign of light ahead, but he was suddenly aware that the walls had ceased. He stopped abruptly, daunted by what he saw. He was in a dark chamber, such as he had left at the other end of the passage. But it was not empty. It was choked with snakes. They writhed in heaps on the floor. They were piled to his own height in fantastic contortions. He moved slightly, and something cold and soft flicked his cheek. He cried out sharply. But even as he did so, he had subdued the first impulse of panic, and had realised its foolishness. It was a vegetable growth that confronted him. Root or branch—he could not tell which. Leafless, vivid, fantastic, writing forms, with pale tints of green or yellow. Advancing upon them, he saw that they entered through an aperture in the wall before him. They crushed in, shutting out all light, almost all air. He wished that he had brought the sword to hack through them. Evidently there was a way out where they entered. He could see no other.

He was excited and eager now to find what the outside might offer. He was in no mood to be deterred by such an obstacle. He laid down the lantern and commenced to clear the way. Inspecting them more closely, he decided that he was confronted by the arms of some creeping plant which, having lost themselves through the window of this chamber, maintained a sickly existence in the darkness.

He found them tough and difficult to sever, and if he pulled as he broke them, a further length would be drawn in, and he had little gain for his effort. But he worked with energy, and soon had his way clear to a window of about three feet square, though he could see nothing through it. The creeper filled the opening, which pierced a wall of rock two or three feet in thickness. Even when he had cleared it sufficiently to discover the limit of its depth, the same growth covered it, a curtain through which no observation could penetrate.

Leaning forward, he worked gently at the screen which closed his view. He was cautious now, not knowing what strange sight might be near him. Finding how thick and close was the obstacle which confronted him, he tried to break more of the impeding growth away, but he was confronted now with the thicker stems of the main growth of the plant. It was a living matted wall three feet thick, with stems as thick as his own thigh, through which he at length worked a sufficient opening for the light to enter.

Lying forward half on the floor of the aperture and half on the supporting creeper, he at last saw the land to which fate had led him.

A wide prospect, several miles in extent, lay beneath and before him. He was looking out from a hillside, not so abrupt as were the cliffs to seaward, yet so steep that it could have been climbed with difficulty but for the vegetation which covered it, which appeared to be of one kind only. The back-sloping side curved, forming to right and left in a gigantic arc, as though the whole island were one huge volcanic crater (as perhaps it had been), and it was draped and hidden from base to skyline in a garment of glossy green, as dark as winter ivy, formed by the giant creeper which flowered profusely with enormous, saucer-shaped flowers of a plumbago-blue colour, and of an overpowering fragrance.

But Charlton's first glance was not upon this garmenting of the rocky wall from which he looked. He had not pushed his way out sufficiently far to see it. He was aware of flat ground two hundred feet beneath him, parrot-green, looking like a grazed field, and beyond that a dark forest of trees, growing close and high, at the sight of which he felt chilled, though the air was warm and windless, for it recalled the forest of which he had dreamed in the night, and which he had feared to enter. There was no beach before it now, but he did not doubt that it was the same, and that the dream had warned him against it.

From his vantage of height he could see somewhat over and beyond the forest, which stretched for several miles before him. Beyond was higher ground, thinly wooded. There was no sign of cultivation, or of the abodes of men, except—far to southward—something shone marble-white in the sunlight. It might be a house or temple. He could not tell.

Encouraged by the solitude of the scene, and reflecting that no creature, human or other, could have been using the entrance he occupied for many months, nor, probably, for a longer period, he pushed further outward, as far as he could do it with safety, till half his weight was upon the branches of the creeper. He saw the crater-like curve of the flower-clad cliff from which he looked. He supposed that it might continue on either hand, until it encircled the island. It must be an island surely! He remained there for a long time, satisfied that he could not be seen either from beneath or above, and watching for any sign of moving life. He heard the cries of seabirds, and of others from the forest. He saw many doves, of an unfamiliar kind, which flew to the hillside. Doubtless they nested in the green-clad wall from which he looked. He thought that he heard the chattering of monkeys. He noticed that the forest had little resemblance to the wooded places of the Pacific islands among which he had wandered. There were no palms of the kind which is most common to those scenes. It was more like the forests of Yucatán, or of Honduras. But yet different. The island could not be of any great size, or it would have been known and populated. It was unlikely that it contained wild creatures of formidable growth. It is not usual to find great beasts in small and isolated islands. Probably, all that he saw might be safely his, to take as he would. Only there was that gleam of distant white, which might mean anything. The heat increased as the sun mounted. Nature drowsed in the heat. Nothing moved.

It was not hot for the tropics. He reflected that the land beneath him must be above sea level. The tunnel had been long, and he had ascended almost all the way.

He became weary of watching a scene which was without incident. He wondered whether he really wished that he should find no companionship of any kind on the island. He might be here all his life. It was likely enough. Atavistic instincts warred within him. There was the desire to possess. There was the fear of the strange tribe. There was the desire of comradeship. There was the instinct of mating. A woman? Yes—in the abstract—he would desire to find one. Any particular one, he might not. He had not yet met one that had the power to hold him. But the stillness gave him confidence, and while he lay and watched, his plans developed. He had no doubt that he could find food here without effort, and in abundance. He knew something of the prodigality of the eternal summer of these tropic isles. Shelter he had already, if there should be seasons of tempest from which to take refuge. *J'y suis, j'y reste,* he said, with a very definite decision. He would not show himself till he had watched many times. There was no haste. He would bring up all the stores from the boat into the greater security of the chamber above it. Perhaps he would bring them here in time. There was time in plenty. A lifetime, it might be. He would do that first and make all things secure, and he would venture out at his leisure. It would be easy to clamber down the sloping wall, with the growth of the creeper three feet thick upon it. He could not fall if he tried. Something moved at the edge of the forest. He had become weary of watching, and did not notice it as it first emerged. It was like a large dog. It was going to a little pool that lay between the trees and the open green beneath him. (Why did the trees end do suddenly? What was the meaning of the bare green level beneath him? his mind wandered to ask.) The creature stood upright, and he saw that he was a man. It went down on all fours again, and he saw that it was a beast. It was in a clearer light now. Men can see far in the glare of a tropic noon. Charlton saw that it had horns on its head. Horns like a goat. It put a bearded face to the water. Having drunk, it rose upright again. Certainly he was a man. Very hairy, or perhaps wearing a coat of skins. And yet the feet were hooved, unless the light deceived him. The creature dropped on all fours again. It disappeared.

Charlton's curiosity was aroused. He would explore that forest when he was ready. The creature, man or beast, had not seemed very formidable. But he would take the rifle when he did so.

CHAPTER FIVE

THE END OF THE *FIGHTING SUE*

Captain Andrew Sparrow of the *Fighting Sue*, pirate, carried on business for twelve years or more in the middle of the last century. He might not have continued successfully for so long a period had he not emulated the caution of the fox, that does not rob the hen-roosts near his own earth. He made his home in the equatorial regions of the North Pacific, which was then a lonelier ocean than it is today. He lay await for his prey in other seas. Then the *Fighting Sue*, Boston-built, brigantine-rigged, with five portholes aside, a long bow-chaser, and two brass cannon on the quarter-deck for use in a flying fight, did not live up to her name unless she were compelled to do so, which was seldom, for she was fast on any wind, and when she hunted, she was not cumbered with cargo. She bullied, robbed, and ran.

She had fought at times, when fight she must—once with a Dutch frigate, from which she had been saved by darkness and a rising sea, with the loss of a topmast and a third of her crew. But escape she did, and with honour of its kind, for Captain Sparrow had handled her well.

When twelve years had gone, he decided that it would be tempting a forbearing Providence too far to continue his operations longer. In this his judgement was sound, as events proved.

His plans had long been made. He did not intend to risk his life by returning to lands that were at one in their objections to the profession which he had followed so successfully. He knew an island where he could retire in comfort. Like most sailors, he desired the land for his later years.

It was an island with many advantages. He believed it to be entirely unknown. It was particularly inaccessible. It was sufficiently large. Its climate was exceptionally good. It was very fertile. He had already made it a place of occasional rest or refuge, and mounted some artillery for the defence of its only landing-place.

It is true that it was inhabited already by a strange and potentially formidable population, but he believed their numbers to be small, and he relied upon the arguments of shot and steel to enslave or destroy them. There were goat-like, half-human animals also, such as he had not seen elsewhere in all his wanderings, but experience had shown him that every land had its characteristic peculiarities, which were apt to be incredible to those who had not beheld them.

He did not only plan for himself. He planned for his crew. He did not intend that any wandering seaman should be in a position to betray him. He proposed that they should land with him, and that the ship should be sunk, so that further wandering would be impossible. He kept this part of his plan in his own mind. He would be the king of a new land.

He had schemed this long, and had perfected the details of his design. He had wealth, but it would be of little use after he had separated himself from the means of spending it.

There was a port in Chile where he was known, and which he could enter in comparative safety. Here he purchased stores of many kinds, and in great quantity. Here he took on board the wives of some of his men, who had made the place a furtive and infrequent home. Lest the port authorities should regard this as evidence that he was not returning, and think it no longer worth their while to grant him immunity under such circumstances, he cut his cable and ran out to sea in the night, when he had taken them aboard.

He made a good voyage, and landed his stores in safety, though with much labour, owing to the nature of the approach to the caves through which he must bear them.

Having done this, the devil tempted him. He had still much gold, and forever is a long time. He was able to think of many things which he might still purchase, of which he had nothing, or of which he might be glad to have more. He determined on a last voyage before he sank the ship.

With the stores which he had put ashore, he left the women and eight of his men. He left also his son, Jacob Sparrow, then a child of ten years. He landed most of his powder. His predatory career was over, and he did not expect to need it.

Before sailing, he invaded the island in force. He made his way through passages which had been cut through the rock to the cliff-tops. He descended the inner side of the cliff, and lost two men in an attempt to cross the bogs beneath it.

Abandoning this design, he continued along the top of the cliffs until he reached the south side of the island. Here he found a safer descent to fertile ordered land. There were some miles of park-like garden-ground, bearing fruits of many kinds, and a luxuriance of tropic flowers. This garden was tended by a number of huge birds, reminding Captain Sparrow of the cassowaries of Patagonia, but much larger. He would have been a tall man who could have looked over their backs, and their heads were nine feet from the ground. Their work was mainly to weed and prune, keeping space for the selected plants, and restraining them to their intended places. They did this most frequently by the simple process of eating that which was redundant. They stirred the soil with their beaks, levelling it with raking motions of their three-toed feet.

Coming upon a number of these monstrous birds, the men looked to the muskets. But Captain Sparrow ordering them not to fire, and the birds neither retreating nor molesting them, but only raising their long necks, and surveying the intruders with sardonic eyes, they passed through quietly.

Beyond the garden they came to a palisade thirty feet high, dividing it from the untamed luxuriance of a tropic forest. The forest was unlike anything which they had seen in Central America, or in the Indian Archipelagos, though it had some characteristics of either. There was a remarkable absence of noxious insects of all kinds. Even in the swamps there had been no mosquitoes.

Turning back through the garden-land, they came to the dark mass of an ancient temple, and to other buildings beyond it. These were closed and silent. Their windows, glazed with a somewhat opaque glass, were high and few, and too narrow for a man to have passed through them. Their approaches were always the same— stairs which wound upwards, steep and very narrow, in the thickness of the wall. He would have been a bold man who would have adventured to climb them without knowing the reception to which the next turn might bring him.

Captain Sparrow waited for three days while there came no sign of life from these dwellings.

He camped in a large hall built of white stone, which was about half a mile from the temple on a slight hill, and which stood open and empty. He had with him a force of forty men, and he had his hands sufficiently occupied in maintaining discipline among them. But he would have no relaxation till he had disposed of the military problem which confronted them. Up to this time he had prudently left the women on board with the remainder of the crew.

He did not allow his men to molest the great birds, who continued their work with apparent indifference, but he gave them permission to shoot some of the little monkeys that abounded in the trees, to demonstrate the nature of their weapons to those who (he felt) were watching them from the silent temple. He also permitted them to invade the forest, where they were mobbed by a troop of the goat-foot satyrs, till they were obliged to shoot one in self-defence. Knowing nothing of mythology, they were not concerned as to whether it were allied either to men, or goats, or gods. They were hungry for fresh meat, after some months of salt junk and ship's biscuits; and they cooked it, as they had done the monkeys, and with results which were even more satisfactory.

Captain Sparrow's patience, often exercised before when he had hove-to for long weeks on a deserted ocean waiting for an expected victim, was again justified when a man emerged from the temple on the morning of the fourth day. Having news of this from a watching scout, Captain Sparrow drew his men into order, and received his visitor with some aspect of dignity upon the lawn which sloped away from the hall of which he had taken possession.

He found himself confronted by a man a head taller than himself, young, lean, dark, austerely handsome, and remote in his aspect. He did not appear to be impressed or interested by the display of disciplined force which met him. His aspect was aloof, but not discourteous.

He did not attempt speech, which would have been obviously futile. He opened a roll of papyrus in his hand, and showed a neatly painted map. With a courteous gesture he proposed that Captain Sparrow should examine it with him upon the long table which ran down the centre of the hall.

Captain Sparrow, who had had other more or less constrained interviews with the masters of the vessels on which he had levied blackmail, many of whom had been unable to speak a common tongue, was quick to accept a suggestion and to appreciate an attitude. Telling his men briefly to stand their ground, he walked in with his visitor to inspect a map which showed the whole island in coloured detail.

Half an hour later, without word spoken or written, they had arrived at an understanding which appeared to be mutually satisfactory. Whether Captain Sparrow intended to observe it, I cannot say.

The visitor (who was the son of the priest of Gîr) produced a duplicate of the map with colouring materials. Swiftly and neatly he painted a space around the temple grounds a dull red. That was to be sacred to his own people. At the southwest of the island a space was painted blue. That was reserved for the privacy of the invaders. Between these, and including the hall in which they stood, was a green space which would be common to both, and in which acquaintance could be made if both parties should desire it. On a waxed blank beneath the map the visitor laid his open hand, impressing it as his signature. He invited Captain Sparrow to do this also, so that the two hands crossed, and he then fastened the map to the wall at the higher end of the hall.

Besides this, Captain Sparrow had learned by gestures, and by swift and skilful sketches, that it would be a cause of difference to continue to shoot the monkeys; that it would be not only such, but in some way dangerous in itself, to molest the great birds; that his people were at liberty to enter the forest when they would and to shoot the satyrs, providing that they did not kill more than one in any one moon; and that there was a stretch of swamp at the north of the island where there was a variety of blue pig, like a small tapir, which they could kill at their own pleasure; and he had signified his acceptance of these arrangements.

He offered drink and gifts of various kinds, but his guest declined them with an aloof politeness, and departed.

Captain Sparrow was a good judge of men in certain relations. He sailed away two days later, confident that the treaty would be honourably observed by those with whom he had made it, and having promised to hang anyone, whether man or woman, who should cause trouble by infringing its provisions while he was absent.

The men that he had left had been chosen by lot from among those whose women were now ashore, as these men were the most loath to start out on a further voyage, and by leaving only such as were married themselves, he judged it the less likely that trouble would arise with the wives who were temporarily deserted, and that those to whom they belonged would be the less reluctant to leave them.

Having ordered all these things with due thought for his people, as a king should, he set out on his last voyage, promising the unmarried men an opportunity at some port of call of remedying their loneliness, if their personal attractions, or the coin with which he would provide them, should prove sufficient inducement to get the women on board.

He sailed with a fair wind for the East Indies—virtuously resisting the impulse to plunder a clumsy merchantman that lumbered away in a very natural panic at the sight of the long low hull, the yawning portholes, the wide spread of canvas, and the flagless masthead—and he was south of the Ladrones when he encountered a succession of light varying winds, which left him drifting on a calm sea over which a heavy mist settled.

The mist cleared during the night, and the dawn, coming with a light breeze from the northeast, showed him Her Majesty's corvette, *Condor*, of twenty guns, about three cables' length distant.

Captain Sparrow was ready for most emergencies, and he opened the game by running a signal of distress to the masthead, and following it, when the inevitable inquiries came, by the announcement that he had had seven deaths from smallpox, and that twelve men were sick below of the same malady.

It would have been sufficient to render many captains disinclined for any avoidable intimacy, but Lieutenant Mainwaring, who was in command of the corvette, was of a sceptical and inquiring mind. He asked questions as to the charter and destination of the brigantine, which were answered fluently enough, but the replies were unconvincing.

The fact was that the vessel showed her character too plainly in every line. She protested her innocence, and it was like a wolf bleating.

Lieutenant Mainwaring, spruce and motionless on his quarterdeck, gazed with an expressionless face at the *Fighting Sue*. He looked at the flag which hung, melancholy in reverse, from the innocent's foretop, and inquired whether it had been there at first sight or had been run up afterwards. There was some difference on this point, but a midshipman (who should have been otherwise occupied) was certain that he had seen it raised as he watched the dim shadow take shape in the dawning light.

Lieutenant Mainwaring signalled, *I am sending a boat*. Captain Sparrow replied with many thanks that he did not need help. Lieutenant Mainwaring smiled slightly, but did not deign to reply.

Captain Sparrow knew that the game was up. So far he had kept his crew below, and had not ventured on any overt preparations for the conflict which was now inevitable, but he had his broadside shotted and run out on the starboard side, which was turned away from the *Condor*. The corvette, having no occasion to conceal her suspicion, had already trained her guns upon the victim of her unwelcome curiosity.

Captain Sparrow watched the approaching boat, and courteously lowered a ladder amidships.

Then, very suddenly, the rigging was alive with men, and the helm went over. There was a cry from the unlucky crew of the boat as they endeavoured vainly to avoid the impact of the vessel's side. The next moment the broadside of the *Condor* flashed and roared. The *Fighting Sue* heeled and shivered as it struck her. There was an outcry of death and wounds on her gun-deck. A round-shot, coming through an open port, caused one of her guns to break loose. It slid across the sloping deck, disabling two who were not agile enough to avoid it.

But the *Fighting Sue* tacked and came round across the stern of the *Condor*, raking her from end to end with a broadside which, though not so heavy as she had taken, was the more deadly in its delivery.

Unfortunately for the *Fighting Sue*, it was a manoeuvre which could not easily be repeated.

Lieutenant Mainwaring, though a very angry man, and handicapped by the necessity of lowering a boat to pick up the crew of the first, who were now struggling in the water, did not allow himself to be flustered. Captain Sparrow had cause to observe, with a natural annoyance, that he was not the only man who could handle a ship efficiently under fire. The *Fighting Sue* was slightly to windward of her adversary, which might have been to her advantage, had she been seeking to close at her own choosing, but it was more doubtfully so when she only sought escape, and to avoid exposing herself to the heavier guns which were waiting to be trained upon her.

With all their canvas spread to a wind which was still too light to give them more than very gradual motion, the two ships showed like contending swans, white on the tropic blue, dodging and twisting as they endeavoured to bring their own guns into play while avoiding the opposing broadsides.

The guns flashed and thundered, and wisps of heavy sulphurous smoke drifted along the wind.

There were few casualties at this stage of the duel, for the fire of either vessel was directed to the masts and spars of her opponent, though with different objects.

Captain Sparrow wished to disable his adversary so that he might put a safe distance between them. Lieutenant Mainwaring wished only to secure his continuing company. So far, chance shook the dice, and threw them when a shot struck the mizzen of the *Fighting Sue*. It did not fall at once, but the next time that the helm went over and the strain came, it snapped off three feet from the deck, and went overside with a tangle of sail and cordage which took five deadly minutes to hack clear so that it floated free. And meanwhile the *Condor* had closed in and was pouring all her weight of metal into the doomed hull of the *Fighting Sue*. After that, only one end was possible. Even could Captain Sparrow have gained his last hope and boarded, it must have been the same in the end. Larger numbers, better discipline, better morale must have decided. But Lieutenant Mainwaring respected the lives of his men, and he avoided every effort which the pirate ship made, like a cornered rat, to get its fangs fixed into the side of its unrelenting opponent.

After a while it lay still on the water like a wounded bird, but the deadly flashes still broke spasmodically from a gun-deck which was slowly sinking toward the ocean level. What use was there in surrender? Yet yield she did at the last, for the powder failed, Captain Sparrow having put too much ashore when he sailed on this peaceful enterprise.

Lieutenant Mainwaring, boarding the sinking vessel, took off nineteen unwounded prisoners, including the captain. He tumbled the wounded men over the side. He was in no mood to be merciful. He had heard of Captain Sparrow before. And his own losses were serious, and were (he considered) the lives of better men. As to the prisoners, acting on the authority given to naval officers in those seas, he held a swift court martial, and hanged them before sunset. He had offered the chance of at least some months of life to any one who would tell him of Captain Sparrow's headquarters. He should be taken home and tried there. He would offer no more. He was not of the kind to make terms with piracy. Yet this slender inducement was sufficient to bring a ready volunteer of treachery, but, unfortunately for himself, the man told the simple truth (excepting only the position of the island, which he did not know), and as it was so obvious that he was lying, he was strung up with the rest, protesting vainly against the incredulity which condemned him. So before sunset they were all hanged except Captain Sparrow himself. It may be that the lieutenant thought he might be induced to speak to better purpose than he supposed that the man had done; it may be that he desired to have some living exhibit to evidence his successful exploit.

Captain Sparrow had leisure to reflect upon the folly of having extended his voyages into the thirteenth year. Being landed in England some six months later, he was tried with more formality that Lieutenant Mainwaring would have considered necessary, but with no less certain issue. He was, however, offered a reprieve if he would give such information as would lead to the recovery of his illicit gains, which were believed to be very great. But this he declined to do. He would not betray his cherished secret, nor the men whom he had left behind. Whereupon he was hanged at Execution Dock.

It may be that he did not trust the promises which were made. It may be that he thought that they would not hang him while he remained silent. It is more probable that he was hanged because there was a degree of baseness to which he would not sink. Which might happen to any man.

CHAPTER SIX

THE ISLAND COLONY

Captain Sparrow had not been explicit as to how long he intended to be absent on his last voyage. He was not one who gave his confidence widely. But he was a man to be obeyed, and as his orders had been that the men he left should proceed to the erection of houses, and should maintain peaceful relations with the earlier inhabitants, they continued to behave with quietness and industry until they had settled down to the routine of their new life. As the months passed, they must have become increasingly doubtful as to whether they would see him again, but there could never have been a day when the uncertainty was changed into the settled fact. They might have thought that he had marooned them with a deliberate treachery, but that was not reasonable, when it was considered that he had left such over-ample stores for so small a colony, with a great treasure of precious things, and had sailed away with an empty hold. Also, he had left his son. It was perhaps fortunate for this youth (as the world esteems fortune) that the possibility of his father's return was in the minds of his companions while he was gaining the years and confidence which finally enabled him to assert himself as his heir and representative. By the time that he did this, the isolated community had settled into a debased existence which was to continue for a generation. There had, at first, been some tentative approaches towards acquaintance between them and the original inhabitants, but these had not been developed. There was an absolute lack of congeniality, of common interests or attractions. But there was a deeper cause. It is the peculiar degradation of Europeans (whether from their carnivorous habits, or other differences) that they have the power to cultivate and harbour diseases which are unendurable by other races. Encountering these for the first time, such people die helplessly.

The surviving race is apt to regard the issue complacently, as an evidence of its superiority. It is as though a sewer should boast that it can tolerate garbage.

The original inhabitants of the island, though they were of apparently finer physique, and of incomparably more equable health, than those who had intruded upon them (having won to this physical condition by a social economy which had systematically eliminated the weakest members of the community), yet suffered, after their age-long isolation from others of their kind, as many inferior races have done in every part of the world when the plague of European civilisation had reached them.

In six weeks more than fifty, out of a total population of eighty, were already dead, including the priest of Gîr; his son, who had negotiated the treaty, succeeding him.

The new ruler, having little faith in the characters, or belief in the goodwill of his new neighbours, and having an additional weight of responsibility on his mind arising from the fact that he had concurred in rejecting the directions of their oracle (which had shown the natural course of events to be that they should have attacked the invaders when first they landed), gave orders that this mortality should be kept secret, fearing that they would be treated with little ceremony on Captain Sparrow's return if he should learn of the losses which they had sustained.

Having no doubt as to the source of the new diseases, he ordered also that all contact should be avoided in the future, and that his people should confine themselves to their own reservation. This not only protected them from further infection, but rendered it the easier to conceal the diminution of their number.

To maintain communication and acquaintance with the course of events, he arranged that he himself (together with his wife, who was his sister also, and who declined to be separated from the danger he incurred) should join the invaders at a feast to be held regularly on the evening of the full moon, and at other times as occasion might arise or inclination lead him.

In doing this, he was influenced by the knowledge that the oracle had foreshown that in the natural course of events, had they attacked the invaders from the first hour with every weapon at their disposal, he himself would have perished among many others; and he was conscious that this had influenced his father to make an effort for peace before appealing to the ordeal of battle.

That effort had been entrusted to him, and had apparently succeeded, but with the result that there were more numerous deaths than would have been incurred in a conflict which would have relieved them entirely of the presence of the white men; and these deaths had not been among the adult males, but most largely among the women and children, which inflicted a more permanent injury upon the community. His father, who would not have died, was dead. He, who would have perished, was still alive. It was not the first time that they had learned that to avoid the future which the oracle indicated was to fall beneath a less tolerable calamity.

Clearly it became his duty to take the risk of any contact with the strangers which might be necessary. And so it became his custom to join them at these monthly festivals, and on some other occasions, eating with them, though without touching the dead flesh, or the foods devitalised by the application of heat, which they preferred. He conversed with them also, learning their language, as they showed no aptitude at his own. This language was a debased form of English, which shrank and degenerated as the years passed, even from the form in which it had been spoken on the *Fighting Sue.* It became blended also with words and phrases introduced by the women of mongrel South American origin who formed the majority of the colony, and quaintly streaked with the phraseology of the Bible, the speeches of Charles James Fox, a book on the breeding and management of cattle, and a collection of broadsheet ballads, which had constituted the fortuitous library of the colony. These books had been read by the more active-minded of the earlier generation, but the younger had shown no desire to read, nor had there been any with the inclination to teach them. The island to which fate had consigned them was of such a nature that the necessity for work was of the slightest. The climate was delightful. Food was abundant. They satisfied their inherited desire for flesh with the monthly satyr, and with the blue pigs in the further marsh.

They soon observed that the restriction in regard to the shooting of the satyrs was a necessity, in their own interest, if the animals were not to be exterminated. As it was, their numbers were not greatly diminished, though it was soon observable that the killing of the younger males resulted in the practice of an increasing polygamy among those that remained. The hunting of these animals constituted the principal diversion of the new colony. The satyrs, having realised the deadly nature of the muskets with which they were attacked, made no attempt at resistance, but fled in a useless terror at the approach of their enemies. They gradually learnt that it was only the male satyrs which incurred any danger, and that it was the younger of these which were most to the taste of their assailants.

The females and young would even continue their feeding undisturbed, the while the hunt went past them, beating the bushes for the hiding males, or breaking into a wild rush or pursuit when they had started their quarry.

Besides these hunts, there were occasional expeditions to the swamps where the pigs rooted and wallowed. But these creatures were dangerous. The women were left behind, and the men went armed with all the miscellaneous weapons they had learned to handle during their piratic exploits. They would return with the heavy carcasses of their victims slung from poles, and more than once with a litter in which a wounded companion would bear evidence of the ferocity of these animals.

After this, there would be an orgy of feasting, ending in a drunken saturnalia, for they had not failed to utilise the possibilities of the grapes which abounded wild in the forest, and hung in even heavier clusters from the cultivated vines of the gardens in which they were free to wander.

The years saw other changes. As the possibility of the return of Captain Sparrow and his companions diminished, the women whom they had left behind attached themselves, more or less definitely, to individuals among those that remained, not without quarrelling and some outbursts of violence, on one occasion with fatal consequence.

The children resulting from these, and from the earlier and more regular unions, were not sufficiently numerous to lead to any excessive increase in the size of the colony. Many of the women were past their first youth, and their lives had not been such as to leave them, as the years had passed, with unimpaired vitality. The island life, in spite of its physical advantages, was not a healthy one, and the children that were born were often neglected or indulged, with detrimental and sometimes fatal issues. They also developed, in some instances, a disconcerting resemblance to the animal population of the island, both in appearance and disposition, the causes of which are very difficult to decide. It would be the simplest solution to conclude that the satyrs were sufficiently near to the human race for a hybrid offspring to be produced, and in support of this supposition it is natural to recall passages in the Mosaic law which indicate that there were nonhuman creatures alive at so comparatively recent a date, toward which some women had a disposition to familiarity, and the character of some of those whom Captain Sparrow had landed would have been of little weight in refuting such a conclusion.

On the other hand, there is no direct evidence to support it, and it is at least equally possible that these physical peculiarities— usually consisting of the growth of more or less conspicuous horns, or of shaggy hair upon the neck and arms, combined with a somewhat goat-like countenance—resulted from the strangeness of the appearance of the satyrs having impressed the minds of these women, whose mentalities would render them susceptible to such influences.

It is an unpleasant fact that the women, mingling freely with the female satyrs, would follow the progress of the hunt, and would combine, with a repulsive, elbowing curiosity, to watch the capture and slaughter of the monthly victim. It seemed that their attitude had gradually affected the female satyrs, until these events were regarded as pleasantly exciting episodes, rather than as attacks upon their kindred by alien enemies, and even the males would emerge from their hiding-places the moment that they knew that a capture had taken place, and watch with an appearance of enjoyment the slaughter and disembowelling of their unfortunate companion.

There was another development which drew a closer link between these people and the half-human beasts on which they fed. They discovered that the satyrs, if caught while very young, could be taught to perform many useful services, and could learn to understand much of the language of their owners, though they made no attempt to speak it.

They captured and reared a number of young females whom they trained to wait on them, and, in particular, to weave a fibrous cloth such as was made and worn by the original inhabitants of the island, and which could be variously dyed, a process for which the forest gave abundant materials, both from its vegetable and insect life.

Another, and perhaps the most potent influence upon the development of the community, was the personality of Jacob Sparrow, after he had arrived at a sufficient age to assert an authority which he found no one prepared to challenge.

A successful leader, whether saint or criminal, must possess certain positive qualities, such as are admirable in themselves, whatever may be the uses which exalt or degrade them.

Captain Sparrow was capable of a cold and calculating brutality, which was sufficiently unattractive. It is difficult to suppose that there are many crimes which he would not have committed, had they been clearly to his advantage. But he had been prudent in enterprise, cool in danger, skilful in manoeuvre, and with a habit of moderation, even in pillage. He had a sense of order and method, and a personal magnetism, which had enabled him to control a succession of lawless crews without permitting licence, or using an intolerable severity. Pitiless in his punishments when the occasion required it, he was never either unreasonable or capricious. He was not loved, but he was both feared and respected. In a way, he was trusted. He had a fortunate reputation.

But Captain Sparrow's son did riot inherit the better part of these qualities. Gross and ungainly in body, he was destitute of physical courage, and averse from physical activity, but he was gifted with a farsighted cunning which enabled him to maintain his position, perhaps more easily than would have been the case had it depended upon the ascendancy of more admirable characteristics. He was neither aggressive nor domineering, and so long as he was not impeded in the gratification of the selfish instinct on which his contentment depended, he allowed his followers a full measure of licence to pursue their own proclivities. He was, however, jealous of the recognition of his position, and insisted upon the wearing of a battered article of naval headgear when seated at the head of a long table at which his subjects assembled, while their own heads were required to be uncovered on those occasions.

He had also an unreasoning cupidity, causing him to cherish many articles which had originally been his father's property, but most of which he did not attempt to put to any service of utility, even had it been possible to do so; and first amongst which were twenty bars of solid gold, each of about two pounds weight, of an extrinsic value of which he had probably gained some knowledge during the early years which he had spent in a South American seminary.

These were always placed in a neat pile upon the table before him. No one ever attempted to steal them, for the sufficient reasons that there was nowhere to which they could be removed to any advantage, nor were they of any conceivable use to anyone who should have been sufficiently foolish to attempt it.

At the time with which we are concerned, Jacob was an obese old man, gluttonous, silent, and somnolent, but still capable of reacting to the excitements of fear or greed, or to any slight upon the dignity of a position which he did so little to justify, under which stimuli he would show that the watchful cunning which had distinguished his earlier years was still sufficient to render his ill-will dangerous to those who should be sufficiently indiscreet to arouse it.

His most amiable characteristic was an unreciprocated affection for a son which had been born to him about twenty years earlier by a daughter of one of the women who had been landed by Captain Sparrow, both of whom were now dead. This son, named Nicodemus by his mother, which had become Demers in the degenerate island speech, was a young man already over six feet in height, of heavy, awkward build, slouching forward as he walked, like a great ape, with long arms and large and very hairy hands.

His hair was long, thick, coarse, and black, growing very low on the forehead. His brows were black and prominent. His nostrils were very wide. His jaw was heavy, with exceptionally large and powerful teeth, over which the lips were never entirely closed.

Over each ear he had a short, blunt horn, about two inches in length, showing at times through the shaggy growth of hair. Possibly his grandmother could have given some explanation of this peculiarity, but it is only right to say that his mother had shown no sign of mixed parentage, and she herself had been attached to Jacob Sparrow with an inexplicable loyalty.

Demers, unlike his father, was of unquestionable physical courage. It was his delight to lead the occasional expeditions against the blue pigs, which were no longer hunted with muskets owing to the powder, too carelessly used by the earlier generation, being nearly expended. On these occasions he would be the only man who could be relied upon to face the savage beasts when they had turned upon their pursuers, and who had the strength and skill to drive home a boarding-pike, while himself avoiding the angry tusks that were directed against him.

Once, when he had been wounded in the leg by one of these animals, he had burst into a passion of uncontrolled ferocity, causing him to batter the dying body of his assailant, and to trample upon it after all life had ceased, until it was flattened out into the muddy soil, and was judged to be unfit to be used for the food for which it had been hunted.

He had possessed himself of three of the younger women of his own generation, without consulting their inclinations, and with these in a bungalow larger than, and somewhat apart from, the abodes of the rest of the settlement, he lived an indolent life of physical indulgence, punctuated by bursts of energy, when he would seize his hunting weapons and rouse his less eager followers to join him. In his own way he was a good husband. He was not bad-humoured so long as his desires were promptly satisfied. He beat his wives, but this was because it gratified his own inclinations and helped to keep him in the good temper which is so necessary for successful domesticity. It was understood that these attentions were a mark of favour, and there is some evidence that the victims were not rendered acutely miserable by consciousness of the weals and bruises with which they were decorated.

CHAPTER SEVEN

THE SEA CHEST

Charlton Foyle carried out his plan with a systematic thoroughness which was natural to him. Many and weary were the journeys which he made to and from the boat. Many were the loads which could only be hauled up with the help of a rope, and that with difficulty. He had found a smooth slab of stone beside the shaft-mouth in the first chamber, to which he had attached no importance previously, though he had stumbled over it on his first landing. He now saw that it was intended to be slid over the opening, which it could cover completely. That was good. But he first found it another use, fastening the rope around it so that he could rest at times when a heavy load was ascending. The day came when the boat was bare of all but the unstepped mast. Even the cordage, the oars, and the heavy canvas had been hauled aloft. Charlton tested the moorings afresh, and left it there at the tide's mercy. He was glad to have it: he might need it again; with half his mind he hoped to do so, but he had chosen the land.

He pushed the heavy slab over the hole. It was too heavy for one man to move it easily, but his muscles had developed as he had toiled. He was conscious of a glow of health and a zest for living, such as he had never expected to feel again. With health came confidence, and it was in a buoyant mood that he prepared for the second stage of the campaign which he had planned.

He had already taken the precaution of ascending the steps that went upward beyond the roof of the chamber which he now occupied. He had found another chamber, similar, but without admittance of any light, and entirely empty. There were drawings on the walls of a character of which he did not willingly think. They were of the same evident antiquity as that in the one where he was now living. There were dark passages leading to other chambers which he had explored without finding their terminations, but he had noticed one thing which contented him. Beyond a certain limit, the dust of time lay on the floors, and it was only his own footsteps which had disturbed it.

He would explore further at another time. That could wait—and the supply of candles for his lantern was limited. So were his matches. He was already calculating and hoarding the irreplaceable things.

The next step on which he had resolved was to convey small quantities of his immediate necessities to the inland chamber, leaving his main stores in the security of the one which he had first discovered, from which he could replace them as he required.

There was a good reason for this—apart from the fact that he did not wish for the added toil of conveying them to the further point—in the fact that, while the first was dry, the second was damp. This change had been observable from the point where the passage had commenced to descend, and in the chamber itself water dripped from the roof at one side, forming a small pool in the inner left-hand corner which must have had some means of drainage, as it did not overflow or diminish.

As he worked, Charlton had debated in mind the advisability of commencing his investigations by climbing up the cliffs rather than down. The creeper would render such an enterprise very easy. He did not think that he was far from the summit. Gaining it, he would have a better view of the island which he wished to explore. He might also contrive some method of signalling to any passing ship, which might be called to his rescue.

But the objections were obvious. Such a signal, were the opportunity to occur, would be equally visible to any unknown inhabitants of the island. He preferred to learn who or what they were before disclosing his existence so freely. To mount to the cliff-top might bring him into an immediate and undesirable notice.

Rather, his mind was concerned to leave his refuge unobserved, and to descend with secrecy. The moon was not full, but it would give light enough, if the sky were clear, for him to climb down and hide at the cliff-foot till the dawn came, and he could see where he went. He recognised that the darkness had its peril as well as its protection. But he did not intend that any living thing should learn of the entrance to his own burrow.

Commencing the last stage of his preparations, he cleared the floor of the second chamber from the creeper that he had torn away to make his passage. It had shrunk and withered, and its bulk had diminished. He would render himself conspicuous by throwing it outward, so he carried it back as he made successive journeys, bringing his food and weapons and some bedding for the drier side of the chamber; and, as he thus cleared the floor and refurnished it, he made a discovery which gave him fresh light upon what was before him, and left his mind in an increased wonder.

It was a seaman's chest of the ordinary pattern. It had been hidden beneath the growth of the creeper, and that which he had torn away had given it a deeper burial. It was unlocked. It contained some clothes, rotten with damp; some tools; some trinkets; two or three books—things that were never of great value except to those who owned them. Some of them were incongruous, as though the possessions of several had been thrown together.

Some of the contents, apart from the mending materials which were in every seaman's chest that the oceans bore, suggested a female ownership. It was easy to conclude that this chest had belonged to one of those whose footsteps he had traced. It confirmed his theory that men had been there at a more recent date than was indicated by the presence of a part of the ordnance of the *Fighting Sue*. It would have given little more information, but for a bulky notebook, which its owner had used for recording his experiences. Charlton seized upon this book with avidity, but it was not easy to decipher, and difficult to understand when he had done so.

It was written in French, which was in itself no difficulty. Charlton had spent two years as attaché to the British Embassy in Paris. He could speak or read the language with equal fluency. But this was the illiterate French of an uneducated man. His constructions were crude, his spelling original. He used words which are unknown to the lexicographer. More serious, he lacked the gift of narrative. He could not appreciate the position of one who was not already familiar with antecedent circumstances. Further, he appeared to have written with a pencil of the poorest quality, and the damp, which had soaked the book, had blurred much of it beyond any hope of interpretation.

Charlton spent many hours over this book, forgetting time and food as he did so.

The one clear thing was a date, written in ink on the first page, with (presumably) the owner's name, *Jean Couteau,* beneath it. The date was less than five years ago. The narrative might be later, but how much later there was no means of telling.

After many hours of study, Charlton summarised the facts he had gained.

At a date unknown, but roughly indicated by the diary, and by the condition of the contents of the chest, the writer, a seaman, had been cast away here, under unexplained circumstances and without means of leaving the island, together with a man named Pierre, sometimes called *le charpentier,* and another man named Latour, with a girl Marcelle, who appeared to have been his daughter. Latour was of a higher social status than the other two men (the narrator called him *monsieur* more than once, and his Christian name did not appear). Possibly he and his daughter had been passengers on a wrecked or abandoned ship. But that was surmise. He wished to sort out the facts only. At the time at which the narrative had been written Jean was alone. The other three had gone into the interior, and had not returned. The girl had gone either alone and first, or together with Pierre. It was not clear whether Pierre had gone in ordinary companionship, or to aid, or in pursuit. He was clearly distrusted or disliked, both by Latour and Jean. Latour had gone after his daughter. He had supposed her to be in some danger. He had asked Jean to accompany him. Jean had refused—from fear. Latour had not returned. Jean had written the narrative at a time when he had no expectation that he would. But, at the last, Jean had resolved to go also. It was not clear why.

There was little more of actual fact that he could decipher with certainty, but there were allusions that implied that the interior of the island was more or less known, as well as feared, by the writer, either by report or observation. That suggested that some parts might be visited with comparative or entire impunity, and that those who had been lost had gone into some further danger. Jean called it an Isle of Devils. That might mean much, or little. The creature which Charlton had seen might suggest a devil to a vulgar mind. Also, he seemed to write under the shadow of a dread which he did not understand, even to be drawn to it against his will, if one blurred page had yielded its secret to Charlton's patience.

Anyway, they were gone, all gone. That was the sinister fact. And yet, was it? They might have found a more attractive location. They might be living now at no great distance. With their help his boat could be manned, and they could make sail for the civilisation that must seem lost forever. They could supply the very help he needed, while he would seem to them an almost miraculous deliverer.

So he imagined, but he did not believe it. There were the things in the chest. They had not been rotten then. They would have been fetched. He believed they were dead.

He looked with a new doubt at the dark line of the forest. There was his dream, and the dread he had felt as he first viewed it. That was a fact—of a kind—also.

But on this day it had no power to daunt him. "Cowards die many times before their death," he said lightly. He would go when the moon rose.

But he took out the cartridges from his rifle, and cleaned and reloaded it very carefully. There had been several others in the boat—heavier weapons—which he had left in the first chamber, but weight counts in a tropic climate, and the ammunition for them was less plentiful. He hesitated over the sword again—but it would be awkward to wear. He had a fantastic thought that he might be flying back for refuge, and find an enemy in possession who might use it against him. Humouring his own folly, he hid it behind the chest.

CHAPTER EIGHT

THE SATYR

Charlton lay down before the short tropic twilight came, and slept soundly. When he woke and looked out through the creepers that screened his window so deeply, the country beneath him was flooded with silver light. It was too much for his purpose, rather than otherwise. His preparations had been made already. He ate a hearty meal of the preserved food with which his boat had been provisioned, longing the while for the fresh fruits which he did not doubt that he would soon pluck at his pleasure. He had filled his pockets with ship's biscuit, for he did not intend to return before the next night, but he hoped to find a meal which would be more to his liking. He slung the rifle over his back, and climbed out.

The stars were brilliant.

The descent was easy. It would not have been difficult had the cliff been perpendicular, with such a thickness of clinging growth to support him. As it was no more than a very steep slope, he could scarcely have fallen far had he designed to do so. He would have sunk among the leaves, and the boughs would have held him.

But he was almost intoxicated by the scent of the great flowers, which came out most strongly in the night-time. He knocked one of them aside, and a night bird—or was it a giant moth?—flew out on silent wings, with a note of protest which was neither hum nor cry, but something strangely between the two.

He slipped a few feet at the last, for the boughs were thicker and less frequent, and the moonlight deceived him; but he was unhurt, and he paused, drawn back under the shadow, in doubt as to whether he should adventure further in the darkness.

It was three hours to dawn.

He decided that it would be best to move cautiously along the foot of the cliff, lest he should betray the locality of his refuge to any watching eyes when the light came. He turned left-hand, for he had in mind that hint of a white building on the distant hill to southward as his ultimate objective, should nothing hinder him earlier. The ground sloped slightly downward from the cliff-foot for a short space, beyond which was the level stretch of verdure that had shown parrot-green in the sunlight. He was of a mind to cross it and gain the wood's shelter now, rather than later. He could lie closely there till the night should be over. But he would continue for a while, and not cross opposite to his own lair. Even a lapwing had too much sense to do such a thing as that.

He trod in a very thick herbage, waist-high in places, and drenched with a heavy dew. The hum of insects was round him, that his steps had brushed from their sleeping quarters. He was glad when he saw that the thick growth ceased and the level plain came to the cliff's base. He stepped briskly forward and his foot sank, and the mud held it. It sank—and continued sinking. He tried to throw his weight back on to the other foot, but it was too late. He had taken a long stride forward, and he could not recover it. He was sunk to the knee now, and the other foot had been dragged forward and was slipping into the slime. He was still sinking steadily. But the foot of the cliff-wall was not beyond the reach of his left hand, and he threw himself sideways toward it. Doing this, he was immersed to the waist. With both arms he grasped the twisted root of one of the giant creepers, which went down into the bog. He struggled desperately against the clutch of the glutinous clinging slime, but it held him firmly. Exhausted to no good purpose, he leaned forward upon the root he held to gain strength and breath. He could scarcely sink further while he remained in that position. To release himself was another matter. But he must avoid panic: there must be some way.

After a long rest he recommenced the struggle, but it was unavailing. The bog held and would not let go.

The firm ground could not be far from his left foot—he was so close to the cliff. If it continued to slope in the same direction?—he tried to move a foot toward it. He could not be sure how far he had succeeded. Very slightly, if at all. But he persevered. Either by that effort, or because he had sunk even more deeply while he struggled, he became aware that the side of his foot was on firm rock. With that leverage to aid him, he worked somewhat nearer the side. He worked the foot somewhat upward. He drew the other foot higher. The dawn was coming before he knew that the struggle was won, and that he was not destined to disappear beneath the green slime that had so nearly engulfed him.

He was safe, and with a feeling of measureless relief at his escape, but he was exhausted and unfit to go further. He struggled forward until he reached a spot where he could rest on ground which was reasonably level, and sheltered from observation. Then he took stock, in the growing light, of the damage which he had suffered. The slime which had held him was peculiarly adhesive. He was still covered by it from the waist downward. From that point he looked as if he had been immersed in a bright green paint.

The clothes which he had worn when he left the schooner had been good and new. They were still in serviceable condition—or, at least, they had been so a few hours earlier, though worn and solid. He had no others. To cleanse them, if it were possible, had become an imperative necessity. But he must rest first. This was something different from his anticipated adventure. He should have been exploring the delights of a tropic forest by this hour, and plucking its pleasant fruits. He realised that to those who go strange ways it is the unexpected that happens. He rubbed his hands with the glossy leaves around him till they were clean of the slime, staining them an enduring yellow with the juice of the leaves as he did so.

Then he examined his rifle. Only the butt had gone under, and having cleaned this, he was satisfied that its utility was unimpaired. His revolver, which had been in a hip-pocket, had suffered more seriously and was beyond any immediate remedy.

The food in his jacket-pocket was but slightly damaged, and he speedily reduced the quantity which would be at the mercy of any further misadventures.

His greatest need was water. Water to drink. Water to cleanse his clothes and boots. Water in which to bathe.

He had the cliff on his left hand and the bog on his right. There was no better course than to go along the narrow space between them, and hope for some improvement in the prospect.

This he did for about an hour. The sun had not yet gained sufficient height to overlook the cliff, and the air was pleasantly cool. So far, there had been no means of crossing the bog, and Charlton began to fear that it might encircle the whole of the interior of the island. He considered climbing the cliff, from the top of which he might have a view which would resolve the doubt. If there were a passage across the bog, he might make better progress toward it above than below. If there were none, the cliff-top would be the limit of his domain. He had had enough of the bog.

While he debated this project there came a change. A narrow space of water showed between cliff and bog. Further, it widened. It was stagnant water, with a thick sediment on its surface of an unwholesome yellow. Patches of rank water-weed showed in places, with a curious iris-like flower of a deep blue streaked with crimson. The whole colouring of the scene was crude, though not discordant.

There were spaces where the bog appeared to have ceased entirely. Shallow, reedy water stretched to the forest. A crowd of gaily coloured waterfowl rose as he approached, and flew northward. Finding a clear-seeming pool, he cupped some water in his hands and tasted it, but it was brackish and very bitter.

The day was becoming hot, and the need of fresh water imperative.

He remembered the pool at which he had seen the creature—man or animal—drinking on the day when he first looked on the land. But that was far behind, and on the other side of the bog.

It was about half a mile further on that he thought it possible to reach the forest. The ground here was irregular. Shallow pools lay in its depressions. Dense canes, ten or twelve feet high, grew on its drier portions. Black mud intervened. In some places, dark pumice-like stones gave a firm footing.

Charlton was eager to overcome the obstacle which held him back from the forest, but the dread of the bog was still upon him. The contending feelings made him at times too venturesome, and at times too cautious. Twice he adventured to cross where the prospect was not attractive. Twice he turned back when it might have been no more hazardous to continue. When at last he crossed, it was to find that he had reached a part of the forest which was so low that he waded at times ankle-deep among rows of trees growing so thickly that there was scarcely space to pass between them.

The ground rose as he advanced. The character of the trees changed. The growth was luxuriant, the colours brilliant. Humming-birds flashed past. Butterflies showed unfamiliar beauties. Great trees flowered like shrubs. Creeping plants festooned them with gorgeous tapestries of blossom. At times the sun, now high in the heavens, broke through the canopy of branches, making a riot of colour around him. At times he walked beneath a rich green gloom, shadowing to a dim twilight where the trees were densest. Straight, lofty aisles opened in places, with long vistas that were beautiful beyond description.

There were paroquets among the branches, and tiny monkeys smaller than squirrels.

Charlton forgot even his thirst for a time as he went through this scene of tranquil opulence. He forgot caution also, till he trod on a yellow snake that bit his boot as he killed it.

He went forward more warily, and with an altered observation. The tiny monkeys ate a nut which grew abundantly. It was a very small nut suitable to their own size, with a brown wrinkled shell. Two would have gone into a thimble. The monkeys pelted each other with shells as they ate. They were obviously carefree and unafraid. They took no notice of him at all.

The nuts were probably wholesome, but they did not attract him. He found grapes which were more to his liking, and ate heartily.

Then he came to a pool.

It lay quiet and cool and deep, and trees grew to its margin.

He had no thought at first except that here was water for his need. Good water, pleasant to taste. He drank freely. He bathed. He cleansed his clothes as well as he was able, drying them in a sunny spot before he resumed them. It was when he was moving along the bank to reach this spot, where he saw that the sun shone, that he came to the drinking-place. It was clear of trees to the water's edge, a gentle downward slope of verdure with a narrow path behind it that disappeared in the forest. The ground was soft at the water's edge, and it was broken by many hoof-marks. Among these he traced the imprint of a human foot. It was small. Not a man's, he thought. Or, if a man's, not that of a European. But it was certainly human.

He looked round. The forest showed no life but that of bird and monkey. He decided to hide, and wait.

He saw that some of the marks were old, and others were quite fresh. It was clearly a regular resort of the creatures of the forest. If he would see before he was seen, here was the place at which to watch.

Bushes grew thickly beneath the trees around the margin of the lake. He made ambush at the side of the path, a few yards from the water's edge, in full view of the drinking-place.

He waited there several hours, lying full length, the rifle before him. The heat increased, and the forest grew silent. He was tired, and it was natural that he should sleep in the stillness.

He was wakened in the afternoon by the noise of a rout of creatures that came down the path to the water.

There were about a dozen of them, old and young, and they made barking, chattering, semi-human sounds that had the effect of a nightmare.

Sight followed hearing, and Charlton doubted that he woke as he watched them.

Manlike in posture when they trotted balanced on their short hind legs—beast-like when they went on all fours, which they did the more frequently—goat-like in horns and hair, and with arms that were more human than those of monkeys—they were the living forms of the satyrs of Phrygian mythology. It would have seemed reasonable that they should dance to the pipes of Pan as they came down to the drinking-place.

Drinking was a formality. A fat, goat-bearded elder approached the waterside while the rest waited. There was a second male, younger, and appearing the more vigorous. He edged up to the water doubtfully. The ancient gave no sign, and he advanced more boldly. The eyes of the rest of the troop were fixed upon him. Suddenly the horns of the elder butted sideways. It was done so quickly, and so entirely without previous indication, that, though the younger male withdrew very speedily, he was not entirely successful in avoiding the attack. A horn caught him beneath the ear. He drew back, snarling, with a spreading patch of red on a hairy neck.

One by one, the rest of the party, which consisted of females, adolescents, and children, came to the side of the ancient, and were allowed to drink while he surveyed them with a goat-like benevolence. But the offender did not venture again until the whole party were retiring. When they had disappeared along the forest path, he drank at his leisure; but having done so, he showed no disposition to follow them. He crept under the bushes on the opposite side of the path.

Charlton lay very still. He could hear no sound. He supposed that the creature had gone, but could not be certain, and remained motionless.

Then he saw the horned head cautiously lifted and withdrawn. There was a look of greedy anticipation in the goat-like eyes. For what was he waiting?

And what was he? A satyr?—or a faun? Charlton was not clear as to the distinction between these two beasts, if beasts were the proper word to use. He thought vaguely that a faun was less objectionable than a satyr, but his mind supplied no data to support this prejudice. Satyr—faun. Satire—fawn. Perhaps an association of sounds and ideas only. But this was trivial. What he did know was that these were creations of Phrygian or Attic myth, blended later, perhaps, with the darker superstitions of Tuscany. He was on an island in the Northern Pacific, in the twentieth century, and these things were unreal. They had never been—like dragons. Dragons! The simile was unconvincing, because he recalled at the next moment that the existence of dragons has been authenticated both by bone and fossil.

"Science" had ridiculed—and then found them. But it had not confessed the error of its incredulity. It had given them a new and longer name, and its omniscient compliance was unruffled by the discovery.

But they were not living. Had not been living for millenniums. At least "science" said so. It elbowed them aside into a remote antiquity. Probably it was right.

But dragons had been only a vague tradition. Widely distributed, it is true, but lacking definiteness, both in place and time. The human mind is so incapable of originality and imagination that this tradition rendered it almost certain that such creatures had been, but that was not a "scientific" argument. Denying their existence, the scientist was unaware that he proved its strength as he did so.

But the traditions of fauns and satyrs are comparatively recent, local, definite. They were also of a kind better adapted for survival in the earth of today, in any place where there were no men to destroy them.

But there was one other objection. Hands and hooves! He had been taught that these were physical characteristics separating the most widely different of the mammalia. They could not be united at the extremities of one animal. But then he remembered the fauna of Tasmania, and its lack of respect for the orderly work of the earlier naturalists.

Nature never did treat the scientists as respectfully as a lady should. She seemed mischievous, almost malicious in the way in which she would play a disconcerting card at the last moment.

Every educated person knew that fauns (or satyrs) did not exist, that satyrs (or fauns) were an invention of the human mind in its childlike infancy—before it had grown sufficiently intelligent to be incapable of imagining anything.

Anyway, here they were. One of them was very much here, and was not wanted. Charlton was quite capable of watching a drinking-place without assistance on the other side of the way.

If he could have withdrawn unobserved, he would have done so. But he doubted the possibility. The ears of the faun (or satyr) were large, and were probably in working order, though one of them might be painful. The old boy certainly knew how to use his horns. Probably this one did also. A...which was it really? Charlton decided that its character must decide. If he observed it in any act of good conduct, it would be a faun. Otherwise not.

Meanwhile, having no confidence in the amiability of its character, he kept his hand on the rifle-trigger. He remembered incongruously that John Wesley (speaking from some experience) had said that he preferred nature to grace in a wife. Probably it was the same with satyrs. But did the question arise?

He was not clear as to what he meant, or whether he had meant anything. He was getting drowsy. He roused himself with an effort. He must not sleep here. But perhaps he had slept? Perhaps he had dreamed the whole thing. It seemed likely. Speculating upon this possibility, he slept, and the heat of the afternoon settled down upon the forest silence like a brooding bird.

CHAPTER NINE

THE DRYAD

Out of sleep he started to an alert consciousness of movement in the branches above him. He looked up, but the foliage was too dense for sight to aid him. He looked out, and the satyr's head rose for a moment in the same curiosity as his own. It might have seen him, but its attention was on that which was approaching overhead. It crouched down out of sight.

Charlton was conscious that, though it was not dark, the intense noon-light had lessened. Shadows moved from the wooded edges of the water. He must have slept long.

A girl leaped lightly from a branch above, and stood at the water's edge. Nude as her first mother in Eden, slim and straight as a birch, she stood with her back to him. Satyrs there might be. But a wood-dryad was beyond believing.

Watching her, he forgot her danger, if any danger were hers. She stood looking out over the pool, in no haste to enter it, the toes of one foot dabbling in the edge of the water.

He could not see her face; and he knew that he could not place her till he did so. But she was not Polynesian. The small head, with its night-dark hair, thick and curling, but cut short to her shoulders, and the slim whiteness of her body, were surely Aryan. They might be English. They might be Greek!

Silent as a cat, the satyr had risen and was approaching behind her.

Charlton's rifle came to his shoulder. He saw the greed of anticipation in the bestial eyes. He saw the heavy paws outstretched, that would have clutched her hair at the next second, and his finger touched the trigger—but he did not press it. The beast was almost between him and the girl, and a shot was too dangerous. He leapt up, shouting to warn her.

As he did so, with a movement almost too quick to follow, the satyr sprang; the girl, wakened by his cry to instant action, slipped aside and leapt upward to the branch from which she had descended. *"Mais non, mon ami!"* she called, with a light laugh, as she gained her shelter. The beast beneath her did not appear aware of Charlton's existence. He stood with raised and clutching hands, screaming and gibbering at the prey he had lost so narrowly.

Cool and mocking, a voice laughed from the green gloom above them: *"Toujours la politesse!"*

Evidently, satyrs do not climb.

Halfway up the tree, bowered in green leaves, and unable to see or be seen from the ground beneath her, the girl paused. She was not concerned about the satyr, though she knew that the escape had been a close one. She knew the hour when the satyrs drank, and had supposed them far away in their sleeping-den when she ventured down to the water. She must be more careful in future. She knew that she was safe from them among the branches. But what was the cry that had warned her? Eyes grew blank as she puzzled it, anxious brows contracted.

A rifle shot broke the stillness beneath her. She knew what *that* meant. There was only one thing it could mean. If *they* had seen her…. She supposed that it was the end, but what could she do but fly to the most remote of her habitations? The stars saw her sleeping, a hundred feet aloft, where a giant tree forked apart and formed a twelve-foot hollow for her hiding-place. An orphan monkey, scarcely longer than a man's hand, that she had found and petted, crept under the warmth of her side and believed itself to be in safety, as a child trusts its parents, who can do so little to aid it, and as a man does not trust God—who can. The girl lay under the warmth of a gathered heap of leaves. There was no better sleeping-place when the skies were cloudless. But she did not sleep; and there was nothing in her heart of the cool gaiety that had mocked the satyr. *If they had seen*—she thought. *If they had seen*....

CHAPTER TEN

THE DUEL

Charlton stood with his rifle raised to his shoulder. He hesitated to shoot. The girl had escaped. The matter was not really his business. There was a half-human quality about the creature before him which his mind allowed as he watched it. He supposed that the satyrs knew nothing of rifles, and this mistake was his undoing. It knew its danger perfectly well. It had seen others of its kind shot down, and the executioners had been unmannerly enough to hang the disembowelled bodies where those that lived could observe them.

The satyr looked at the rifle, and its fear was abject. It did not attempt flight, because it knew that it would be useless. But the shot delayed, and a wild impulse of resistance woke in its frightened mind. Charlton, seeing the terror which he inspired, expected it to turn and run.

Instead of that, it ducked suddenly and ran in under the rifle. It was about six paces distant when it did this. Charlton lost half a second from sheer surprise, and when he brought his rifle down, the beast was immediately beneath it. He shot it through the loins, the muzzle almost touching the hairy skin. At the same instant the butting horns caught him. He felt a sharp pain in his left thigh, as he drew back from the creature, which had collapsed on the path. He looked down, and saw that he was bleeding freely.

The satyr (he was sure that it was a satyr now) rose on its hands, and dragged itself under the bushes, its hind-legs trailing.

Charlton knew that the ground rocked beneath him. His leg was failing. He must not faint, he told himself, till he had stopped the bleeding. He must not. He was back in the bushes now. It was bleeding fast, but he was satisfied that the main artery was untouched. The wound was about three inches above the knee. He tied a piece of string tightly round the leg, immediately above it. It was the best he could do. Then he lost consciousness.

Under the bushes on the other side of the path lay the satyr. They had both returned to the places from which they had watched the water. Fate laughed, and the forest resumed its peace.

CHAPTER ELEVEN

THE NIGHT

During the night Charlton regained consciousness. But he could not think clearly. He had been dreaming of a girl who stood about to bathe at a lakeside in a tropic forest. A delightful scene, but not such as is familiar to the waking mind. His dream was mixed with wild imaginings of satyrs, horned and hooved, which he knew did not exist. He was too sane to believe it, but the dream was very real. When he tried to think of where he really was, his mind failed and wandered. He remembered that he had planned to explore the forest tomorrow. But what were the branches overhead tonight, and the star that showed where they parted? He must be dreaming still. He wished he could return into the dream entirely. But his mind wandered. Why did she not turn her head? It was always so with dreams. Anyway, he was tired now. He would sleep.

* * * * * * *

But the girl did not sleep—because she was not sure. There are few griefs or terrors which can resist sleep in its due season. A murderer can sleep, though he know that he will be hanged in the morning. But not if he be in doubt whether he will wake to death or a pardon.

She had lived safely for two years. She knew that they believed her dead. She was safe in the trees. Doubly so since she had made friends of the little monkeys, who could warn her while they were a mile away. But anyway, they only came to hunt the satyrs, and that only once in every moon. She was always safe in the trees. Even the climbing snakes did not molest her.

But if they had seen! And they *must* have seen, or who should have cried to warn her? And yet—there was something strange. The time—the place—the voice—she was not satisfied, though her reason told her that there was only one explanation, and her fear confirmed it. No less, she was resolved to go back to the spot when the morning came. Reason told her again that she should be as far from it as possible. She had a range of about ten miles of forest. About ten square miles of trees that grew so close that you could go all the way through a green cover without sight of earth or sky. Surely she could defy them to find her! And with the little monkeys to warn her. But she knew that she would be hunted—hunted—and there could be but one end.

She had lived for two years in the forest. Food was abundant. She had a score of shelters when the rain came. And there had been no storms such as she had been taught to expect in such latitudes. It was a land of continuing peace. There was little cold, even at night. And the sleeping-shelters she had constructed or adapted were ample for her needs. She had had leisure to make them. They, and the continual watch against discovery, had been all she had to keep her mind alert. But she had not been unhappy. At least, not after the first weeks. She had learned to know the forest. How much she had learned of beast and bird and insect, of tree and herb and creeper! And health, such as she had never known or imagined. Health that made life a joy unspeakable, as she moved from branch to branch, or stretched lazily in the sunshine.

Well, it was changed or over now, and she was sure of one thing only. She must know. So she went back in the morning.

CHAPTER TWELVE

MARCELLE'S TALE

The satyr was dead. He lay face downward, as he had crawled under the bushes.

The sudden tropic sun had not risen, and the westward stars still showed in the reluctant sky when the branches moved and the girl dropped lightly to the ground beside him.

She had no doubt that he was dead, though she kicked a shaggy side with her foot to prove it. Cold and stiff. There was no doubt there. But having shot him, why had they left him thus? They hunted for food. He could not have escaped their notice so easily. He had not gone twenty yards from the spot where he must have been shot. And he had left a trail of blood as he moved. She traced it backward. There was a mystery here, and it was vital to her to solve it.

On the open path she could see where he had fallen. The light was still dim, but her eyes were keen, and she saw that there was another trail of blood which went the opposite way. Swift as a startled bird she regained the branches, and was high in the forest roof before she would pause to consider it. She did not know what it could mean, and she had learnt the first law of the forest life: that what is not understood is to be avoided swiftly. She had descended dangerously to obtain knowledge, as a bird will swoop to snatch the food it needs, but she would consider it in safety.

She considered, and found it inexplicable. There had been only one shot. Possibly it might have hit two of the satyrs, and in following one they might have lost the other.

It was possible—but unconvincing. And there was the cry that had warned her. Besides, they did not hunt singly, nor, in her experience, had they done so at such a distance when the light was failing. She was sure that there was something here which she had not discovered, and which she must know for her peace of mind, if not for her safety.

Very cautiously she descended again. Among the trees that met overhead, she crossed to the other side of the path. Then she descended to the lower branches. She found Charlton easily. After the first restless hours he had fallen into an easier sleep, and the movements in the boughs above did not disturb him. She watched him for some time, and when assured that he slept, she dropped silently to the ground. Her feet made no sound on the soft verdure as she approached. She bent over him, looking at his wound. She did not think it serious. A very cool and tearless Aphrodite, she considered an Adonis who would not die. At least, he would not die of that wound. There were other possibilities. She saw that he was a stranger who had doubtless been cast upon the island, as had herself and her friends. He might be alone. If so, he would not live long were he discovered. He must be warned. Also, he knew of her existence, and if he were caught, he might tell it, thinking no evil. For every reason he must be warned. She looked searchingly at the sleeping face. Was there a possibility that a road of escape was opening? Or that here was a companion for her loneliness? Her eyes sought every detail of his equipment for guidance. She learnt that he had come through the bog. That meant, almost certainly, that he knew nothing of the dangers which threatened him. But she must not risk anything till she was surer. And, in any case, he must not see her like this.

Quietly, as though her thoughts had penetrated to his sleeping mind, he woke, and their glances met for an instant. Startled into full wakefulness by the apparition, he raised himself and looked round, but there was no one in view. He was not sure that the delirium of the night had left him.

Then the pain of his wounded leg gave him a more urgent consideration. The horn had ripped the muscle for an inch or two, but he did not think it had gone deeply. It was less serious than he had thought, though it had bled so freely. But his leg was numb from the way in which he had tied it. He cut the string, and the blood forced its way back into the deserted veins. The wound did not break out again, but he was afraid that it might do so should he attempt to walk. Yet drink he must. His thirst was maddening. He crawled down to the water.

Having drunk, he washed and bandaged the wound. He went back into the bushes. Not wishing to meet the satyrs again in his present condition, he withdrew further from the path. He still had some food, and the night having been warm and dry, he was little the worse for his exposure. The curse of the mosquito had not fallen on this lonely island. He would rest today and hope that he should be able to proceed quietly tomorrow. He had seen nothing yet that he need fear. The satyrs were not formidable. He realised that he had been attacked from desperation rather than courage or ferocity. But the vision of the night before would not leave him. He was determined to find her.

He drowsed as the day advanced, though with a mind alert for any sound that might rouse him, and with the rifle near to his hand. He did not think that he had slept heavily, and was surprised to find that a large bunch of grapes, a pile of guava fruit, and a red variety of banana were beside him.

They were welcome in the heat of the afternoon, relieving thirst and hunger, but they were more than that. They were an evidence that he was overlooked, and by those who were not unfriendly. Perhaps he should take them as no more than recompense for a warning cry.

He remembered that he had not seen her face. The waking glimpse had been too vague and transient for any enduring impression to be left on his mind, though he sought it vainly. His heart beat faster as he recalled the vision in the tropic twilight of the previous day. Certainly he would find her.

Night came, and it was very dark in the forest. Having rested during the day, Charlton now felt sleep to be impossible. His mind besieged the problems that the island offered, but found no point at which he could penetrate to their solution.

While he wondered, a voice called low and near through the silence, *"Dormez-vous?"* He was uncertain of the direction from which it came. There was a rustling in the leaves above him, but that might be the monkeys. He answered in English: "No. Who are you?"

"I thought you were…," came the cryptic answer.

"Si vous—if you mean I'm English," he answered, "you're right, but I can speak your language if you prefer."

"Oh, they're both mine," the voice answered, "and I've forgotten them about equally. We'd better keep to yours. But I'll tell you who I am, if you'll lead the way."

"Well, I asked first," he said, not unreasonably.

"But I'm a girl, and can't wait."

"Are you the one that escaped from the beast I shot?"

"I may be; but I shan't speak again till—"

"Very well," he said, resigning himself to the unavoidable. "But there's nothing to tell. My name's Charlton Foyle. My age is twenty-six. My height, five feet, ten inches. My weight varies. My profession is (or was) that of a junior attaché. The doctors say I am ill, and I thought they were right; but I'm beginning to doubt it. I drifted here in a boat that I was too weak or too stupid to handle. That's the whole tale, and now will you please explain—everything?"

"You have a boat?" The question came breathlessly. "Where is it?"

"I'll tell you if you'll play fair. You haven't answered my question."

"There's really nothing to tell," the voice mocked him. "My name's Marcelle Latour. My age is twenty. My height is five feet, six. My weight varies. My profession is difficult to define. The doctors might have said I was ill had there been any to consult, and had I asked their opinions. I drifted here on a raft that I made no attempt to handle, as I was both too weak and too stupid. Also, there were others with me who were more competent. That's the whole tale, and now will you please explain—where is the boat?"

"The boat's quite real," he answered, "and quite safe." His mind was divided between a reasonable caution and an instinctive confidence. "But it is too large for any one man to handle. If your companions are anxious to leave the island, we might do so together."

The voice that answered had a new note of seriousness. "I have no companions. They are dead. I am quite alone. No one knew that I was alive, till you saw me. But if you have a boat, it may be life for both of us, if you will take me. I must tell you all, and you will understand when you hear. But if you don't believe me, please say, and I'll stop. I don't suppose you will. But you may because you've seen something—" She hesitated, as though hardly knowing how to commence. Memories crowded back as her mind turned to the past. Charlton had leisure to wonder how near she was, and to recall the vision which his mind held, so that he hardly heard the first words in which she began her narrative.

"It was two or three years ago—I can't say more exactly—that I was travelling home with my father—he was French, but my mother was English. He had been on a scientific mission to the French islands in Polynesia on behalf of the Government. We were run down by another ship in the night. When the morning came it had sunk, or was out of sight—I don't know which. They said it was damaged more than we were. Anyway, we were sinking. Some of our boats were smashed, and most of the men went off in two of the others. The captain and four of the men stayed. He advised us not to go with the boats. He thought the ship could be kept afloat, and that the risk was greater if we left it. The weather was very rough.

"But the ship sank during the next day, though not till the men had made a large raft, for the only boat we had left was a very small one. They said the raft would be safer. They made it with a mast and sail. It was large and strong, and floated high on the water. We had loaded the boat with provisions and towed it behind us. It was better weather by then. I don't think I was very frightened. The ship went down so gently that the raft floated clear of the deck before it really sank. But the weather got worse again, the rope broke, so we lost the boat. We were on the raft for about three weeks. The last week we had water, but no food. We caught fish, and one of them must have been poisonous, for the captain and one of the men died. It was a horrible time.

"Then we saw the island. We thought we were saved at first, but when we got near, it was all high cliffs with no landing-place. We sailed too close in, and were beaten against the cliff, and one of the men was drowned, and the raft was damaged. We were too weak to do much to save him. Then we found a kind of tunnel in the cliff. There was a ledge along the side on which we landed."

"Yes, I know the cave," Charlton said, "you needn't explain that."

"Very well," she answered, "if it's the same. Anyway, that's how we got here. We saved a few things, but couldn't get the raft properly in, and it went out to sea when the tide turned. Most of our things went with it.

"We climbed up some steps of a kind—you know them?—and lived for weeks in the rooms above. We hauled up the two chests we had saved.

"Two?" he said. "I only saw one."

"There were two chests," she said, "but they don't matter. We were very weak, and we had no food. We found a way out on the inner face of the cliff. It goes all round the island like the sides of a cup. Perhaps you know the way we found? Very well. We all felt afraid, but Pierre Janot ventured out and he came back the next day with plenty of fruit, but with a tale that he had nearly died in a bog, and of such strange creatures that we were more afraid than before."

Marcelle paused for a moment, as though doubtful how to continue—or reluctant to explain all that had happened—and then said: "I must tell you about these men. Jean Couteau was quite harmless. He was like a dog that is faithful, but too timid to be of any use to help you in danger. He had religion. He trembled at the tales that Pierre told us. He thought that we were on an island of devils—he wasn't far wrong in that.

"The things Pierre told impressed my father very differently. He was interested, and questioned him closely. But he didn't like Pierre, and he was absorbed for these first days in examining the drawings and other things in the upper rooms?"

"The upper rooms?" Charlton interrupted.

"Yes—haven't you seen them? That is where he had the chest taken that held the papers. Well, it doesn't matter.

"But after a time Pierre's tale changed. He said that he had found the people who really controlled the island, and they were quiet and friendly. Why should he spend his time bringing us food by such a path, while we could get it ourselves in safety?

"We should have had to venture out ourselves, had he refused to do so. He said he hadn't told them where we were hidden, out of respect for my father's wish, but that he should not return again unless one of us would go with him. When he said this my father was not with us. I did not want to go alone with him. There were reasons. But I was very tired of the caves, and I wanted the forest. Also, I thought that, if he did not return, it would be useful for one of us to know the way he had found for crossing the bog.

"He said that I could be back within a few hours if I wished. I was not really much afraid of him. Anyway, I went.

"I had made Jean promise not to tell my father till I returned, but he was frightened and did so almost as soon as we had started. My father followed. He kept us in sight, though we did not see him.

"Pierre led us to the people who live at the end of the island. It's no use telling you about them. No one would believe who has not seen them. They are not beasts. They are men—of a kind.

"He led us by an indirect way, so that we entered their village from the further side, and they were between us and the nearest way of retreat when first we saw them.

"They were crowding round us in a moment. They must have known we were coming. They talked in a language which is difficult to understand, but which has many English words. I think they would have pulled me to pieces out of a kind of savage curiosity—I am sure they would have tom my clothes off me."

Marcelle stopped suddenly, as though the allusion brought a sudden self-consciousness of the present, but resumed in a moment.

"Pierre shouted to them a warning about 'Demers,' at which they seemed to hesitate, and it was just then that my father joined us. They seemed half frightened of my father, and drew back a few steps. There must have been fifty of them, men and women and some half-grown ones. You couldn't think of them as children. It was like being awake in a nightmare.

"Only my father being there gave me some confidence. He was never afraid of anything. I saw him looking at them as aloofly as though they were a new species for him to classify. They felt it somehow, and hung back like a lot of cowardly wolves, each afraid to be the first to spring at us.

"Then there was a cry that Demers was coming and—well, I can't tell you what he is"—Charlton heard the shudder in her voice as she named him—"he's the son of the old man who rules them.

"He took us to him, in a white stone hall that these creatures could not have built. My father talked to me in French, which they could not understand. 'I don't think they are cannibals,' he said, rather doubtfully, 'but in any case we shall know how to deal with them. They have no intelligence.' He asked me to interpret what they said, as far as I could understand it. He could write English well, but not follow it when spoken, as I do, and they did not speak any proper language at all.

"The old man is called Jacob. Even my father would not say that he has no intelligence. When we talked to him, we soon knew that Pierre had betrayed us. I don't know why he did it, unless it were out of revenge because I had shown I disliked him. You might understand if you knew him. He is still with them. But, of course, he does not know that I am alive.

"We found that I was to be a wife for Demers, and I should have been handed over to him without ceremony as soon as Jacob had seen me, but for my father's contrivance.

"He did not try to speak to them himself. He told me to tell them that he could not speak their language. They gave us time to consult, and to exchange words in French which they could not follow.

"My father told me not to look frightened, as there was nothing to fear. I was to tell Jacob that I was quite willing and that he approved, but that there was a prophecy that, if I were married on any day except when the moon was full, my husband would die within a week. It was the kind of idea which would come to my father's mind, and we must have acted well, for they believed us at once. It was four days before the moon would be full.

"Pierre could not have believed the tale of the prophecy, but my father told him that he had considered that, as there was no means of escaping, it was the best thing that could happen that I should be married to the son of the chief man of the island. Pierre seemed puzzled and sullen, but our manner must have convinced him. As soon as we were alone, my father told me not to be afraid. 'Of course,' he said, 'I shall not let that ape touch you. But we have four days. For the next three days don't even think of escaping from them. Just forget the future. I shall be ready with a plan when the time comes. Meanwhile, I want to gain their confidence and look round and learn what I can.'

"My father was like that. Nothing worried him needlessly. He was always sure he could deal with it, and I had learned to trust him. And for the next three days he seemed absorbed in the strange things that were around us. I think, had he really been in the hands of cannibals, he would have been capable of forgetting his coming fate, had he been interested in the shape of the pot which they put on to boil for the coming meal.

"They gave us each a hut, and while within these we were quite free, and more or less private, and they did not exactly guard us when we were out, but they followed us about, so that to escape unnoticed would have been impossible. We might have tried it in the night, but I knew my father was planning better than I could do, and I just did as he told me.

"It is a wonderful place, like a great garden. But the gardeners are huge birds, taller than men. They call them rukas."

"Birds?" Charlton's voice was incredulous.

"Yes, I knew you wouldn't believe without seeing. But they don't belong to the people of whom I am telling you. Beyond them there is a great red temple, where there are others of a different kind. We learnt that they reserve part of the cultivated land to themselves, and we were warned not to enter it. But the great birds go where they will. They are like ostriches, but larger—and different. My father said they were a kind of giant cassowary, till he looked at their feet. He smiled when I spoke of ostriches, and asked whether I did not know that those birds had only two toes. But when he looked at their feet he said they were different from cassowaries, but they were more like them than the rhea. They looked down at us in a way I didn't like. It was as though we amused them. But they did us no harm. There were other strange things, but it's not easy to tell them. It would have been beautiful, but for the horror.

"On the second day they took us with them to hunt a satyr which they wished to kill for the wedding feast. I needn't describe that. It made us realise the kind of beasts that had caught us, more than we had done before. I've watched many others since, but it was new then. Of course, we all eat things that are killed—at least I used to—I haven't here—and we may enjoy chasing them, but it was the way they killed it after it was caught—one of them shot it and broke its leg—the way they gloated over killing it, and crowded to see and share, that was so loathsome—I can't describe it."

"Shot it?" Charlton interrupted again. "I thought you said that they were only half human, and I supposed this island to be unknown to Europeans. Have they got firearms?"

"They have got some muzzle-loading muskets, and large clumsy pistols. My father said they were half a century old—and a whole lot of swords and other weapons. Didn't I tell you they spoke in a half-English language? They say their ancestors came here in an English ship. But they're not English now—they don't seem quite human. You need to see them to understand."

"Well, go on. I'm sorry I interrupted."

"There isn't very much more to tell, and the time's passing. I must go soon," Marcelle answered. She knew the hour of moonrising, and had no intention of being seen when its light should flood the glades of the forest, and give a glimmering twilight to its recesses. "The boundary between the gardens (which are like a great park with lawns and fruits and flowering trees and creepers) and the forest in which we are is a high palisade, too strong to break through easily, even should any creature wish (the satyrs would never dare the attempt), but there is nothing more than an open pathway leading to a gate in the palisade to divide the gardens between the two races that share them. My father was bent on seeing the temple, and he may have thought that we should find some protection among people who were apparently respected by our captors. He told me of his intention, and asked me whether I should prefer the risk of going with him or remaining. I chose to go.

"So on the third day we just walked over the boundary. They cried out in anger or alarm—there were a dozen of them around us at the time, but the movement was unexpected and they did not dare to follow. They kept shouting to us to return, till a drop in the ground hid us, but we took no notice.

"We went on for a mile or more in absolute solitude, getting quite near to the temple. It is neither beautiful nor ugly, except as strength is beautiful. It gives an impression of being immovable, though the world should fall from beneath it. It is very squarely built and of great size, but the strangest thing is its colour, which is red, but of a very deep, almost purple tinge, and of an extraordinary intensity, so that you feel that it is not merely on the surface, but all through the great square stones that build it. You feel that it is soaked in this colour. I remember that I felt awed as I looked, and a more sinister impression, which I could neither shake off nor explain.

"As we looked, a priest came from the temple toward us. He was tall and dark, of a quite different race and character from those among whom we had been. He looked at us in a remote, austere way, but without hostility. When he spoke I was startled to hear him use the language to which I was becoming accustomed. He must have learned it from them but, as he spoke it, it had lost its vulgarity. He did not rebuke us for trespass, he simply told me to stay where I was and await my father's return. He signalled with his hand to one of the rukas that was near us, and it came and waited beside me. My father went with him. It was near twilight when he returned.

"We had walked most of the way back before he spoke, and then he was different from anything which I had known previously. He was always cool and sufficient, but he spoke now very slowly and with an unusual gravity. He told me that the priest had shown him strange things, but he could not repeat them. He said, 'I have seen what is going to happen during the next days, and some things that are further. I want you to remember that if you have courage, all will be well.'

"I said, 'Will it be well for you also?' and, as he did not answer quickly, I continued. 'But if you have been warned of any danger, surely we can find some way to avoid it.' I had a fear that some tragedy was upon us from the tone in which he spoke, and a restraint that was different from his usual serenity.

"He answered, 'Yes, we could alter it. No one can really foresee the future, because it is subject to incalculable influences. It is not fixed beforehand. But—I think I have seen what will happen if we make no move to avert it; and if we do that there may be a worse alternative. That is the danger. Against that the priest warned me before I looked. If I should tell you, it would not happen, and you would only think that I have been credulous of folly. In any case, it may not. Many chances may avert it. But it might be worse.'

"After that he would say no more for some time, and then he turned to me and said, 'I want you to promise that you will never consort with this canaille, whatever happens. Anything would be better than that. You must have patience as well as courage.' I could not understand then, though I gave the promise he asked, but those words have shown me since that he really must have seen, and that he gave up his own life because he saw that it would mean escape for me if he let things happen in that way.

"There was great excitement over our return, and an increased suspicion and watchfulness. I was questioned as to our experiences, and replied on my father's advice that I had not gone far, and had seen nothing. I did not mention that he had been in the temple separately.

"The next day Pierre came to us with a proposal that we should escape together. We had good reason to distrust him and my father replied that he saw no hope in escape, and had no intention of doing anything of the kind.

"We learnt that they had no proper marriage ceremony, either religious or other. But a feast was held once every month in the great hall on the night following that on which they hunted the satyrs, and it was their custom to have a kind of dancing orgy after this feast, which would fall on that occasion upon the day my father had mentioned, when the moon was full.

"My father told me to say that he would hand me over to Demers at the conclusion of this feast, if he could have a house built for his own use, and if it were agreed that I should be the head wife, whomever Demers might marry afterwards; for we noticed that some of them had two or three wives, though that was not general, for the men and women were about equal in number. My father made some other conditions—I needn't trouble to tell them—but, while they were not difficult to grant, they gave an impression that we were quite agreed to the marriage, which was no doubt what he intended.

"Anyway, I don't think they had any suspicion.

"My father told me his plan, which was so simple that I was afraid at first, till I saw that he was right, and that its unexpectedness would be its strength. He said that, as the evening passed, they would all get more or less drunk, and that he would give me an agreed signal, either while the feast should still be in progress, or even on the way to Demers' house afterwards, at which we should quietly escape among the trees by a path which we agreed, and which we both memorised very carefully.

"He pointed out that they would be more or less unarmed and taken by surprise, even though they might still have control over their wits and legs, which he thought unlikely. He had a revolver which he always carried, though he was not in the habit of showing it, and I doubt whether even Pierre knew of its existence. He said that we could easily outdistance a scattered pursuit as we should have a clear objective, and that, when we reached the caves, we could defend the entrance, should they follow and find it. I said that Pierre would betray that, to which he answered that he would deal with him, but he did not say how. I think they must have known more or less of the caves, as their ancestors appear to have come by the same way, but they may have forgotten them, or lost knowledge of the entrance.

"He told me all this with evident confidence that the plan was sufficient in itself, but yet as though it were of no real importance one way or other, and his mind was preoccupied with something of a greater significance, but he said no more.

"I think it would have all gone as he had planned, but, when the feast had just started, and we were all seated at the table, Jean Couteau ran into the hall.

"The old man Jacob and his son were at the head of the table, and we were at his right hand, the priest and his wife—I suppose they were guests to honour the occasion being opposite to us. I had seen my father and the priest exchange glances, and look toward the entrance of the hall, which was at the further end, more than once, as though they were expecting some thing to happen. When Jean appeared, I heard my father say to himself, 'Donc c'etait vrai?' and then very quietly to me, 'Come at once; it is now or never.'

"Jean ran into the hall crying something about hell and devils, and waving his arms I think he was quite mad—and at once the whole hall was full of screams and outcry. They are a people that can be roused to a frenzy of cruelty or excitement in a moment. It is the same when they hunt the satyrs. They sprang at Jean as though they would tear him to pieces with their hands. Some of them wore cutlasses—they have a lot of old ship's weapons—and they drew them and slashed at him while he dodged wildly about the hall. I don't know why his coming made my father decide that we must go at once, but we could have done nothing to save him. The way he screamed was like putting a match to a laid fire. I saw him killed before we were down the hall.

"We rose so quietly, and the attention of everyone was so much taken by what was happening at the further end of the hall, that we were halfway down it before any effort was made to intercept us. I looked back once and saw the priest watching the confusion as one who looks at a play which does not concern him. Then I caught the old man's eye, and knew he had seen us. His son had half risen, and he was holding him back with one hand, and saying something to him very urgently. I think he saw the revolver in my father's hand.

"Then he shouted something which I could not hear, and at once attention was directed toward us. We were walking down the side of the hall. I was nearer the wall, with my father on my left, and the backs of the people—men and women seated together were at his left side. They turned and saw us, and began to jump up to stop us. My father quickened his pace. He did not fire, though one or two of them drew their cutlasses as they turned, and thrust at him as he passed them, but, as we were near the entrance, a man sprang in front of him and seized me by the arm. I shall never forget his face. He pulled me in front of my father, and I struck at him with my free arm. He screamed out something—for the others to help, I think—as he did so, and I think I screamed in a different way. It must have been a wild scene. I think my father was the only one there, besides the priest, who kept his self-control. I saw the man's black eyes mad with excitement, and his teeth, very white, and snarling like a wolf, and then my father fired over my shoulder, and the face fell.

"The next moment we were clear of the hall, and running hard for the way we had chosen.

"We could not reach it. They were close behind and around us. Some of them could run faster than we. But they were afraid to come close. My father fired if they did, aiming deliberately. I don't think a shot missed. So we gained the trees and a moment's safety, but we were cut off from the way we had intended—the safe way back across the bog. In the shelter of the trees my father stopped a moment to reload. Then I noticed that his left arm was bleeding. I asked if we could not wait to bandage it, but he said no—it was nothing—and hurried me on. 'It's not the arm that matters, it's the side,' he said, and I saw that he had been wounded there also. It must have been before we got clear of the hall, when they were thrusting at him with their cutlasses. I don't know how deep it was: I suppose he knew that it would make no difference in the end.

"We came out of the wood to an open space that sloped down to the bog. It was open water in places, and smooth green mud in others, and there were great patches of reeds with gaudy blue flowers striped in mauve and crimson. I expect you have seen them.

"They were close behind us then, and closing in on either hand. They drove us down to the bog. We crossed it for some distance, walking heavily, but not sinking. They seemed afraid to follow. We made for what seemed like an island of reeds, but, when we were near it, we found a clear space of water about twelve feet across which separated us from it. My father said, 'You can swim better than I. Could you swim round to the further side and see whether we could land there? Slip into the water as though you were sinking in the bog.'

"I was afraid, but I did not like to refuse. I was used to obeying him. I did not understand his purpose. I slipped down as he said, and swam low till I was out of sight of those who were pursuing us. Then I climbed into the reeds. I pushed through cautiously till I came to where my father was still standing, but he had sunk to his boot-tops in the thick mud. I called to him cautiously that there was a safe way round, but he answered without turning to me that he had a different plan. He was drawing his feet out of the mud with some difficulty as he did so. He spoke again without looking toward me, 'Make for the forest; it will be safer than the caves. Do not answer.' Some of our pursuers were following doubtfully a little way into the bog, and my father fired again, and one of them fell into it. The others tried to drag him out, but found they were being drawn in and let him go. They were all watching him sink, and could not control their excitement as he screamed to them to rescue him. They broke into a kind of nervous laughter. They seemed to be frightened, and yet to enjoy watching him. It held my attention till he disappeared, and then I saw that my father had moved some distance away, as though he were making for another patch of reeds. Then I saw that three men were running down to the edge of the bog with muskets. They fired at him all at once, and he fired back twice. I didn't think they had hit him. I saw one of the men had dropped his musket, and was holding both hands to his body. When I looked for my father again he had disappeared. I never saw him again. He may have been hit, or he may have sunk in the bog. I lay still. I was too frightened to move. There was a crowd at the edge of the bog by this time. The old man and his son were with them. They were all talking and pointing. I suppose they thought I had sunk. I don't think any of them would have been brave enough to come to search after watching the one that sank.

"They went at last. It was sunset. I lay there too frightened and too wretched to move, till the moon was high in the sky. The night was as cold as they ever are on this island, and I must have been drenched by the swim, but I did not notice. It was the coming of a snake that started me. It swam through the clear water with its head raised in the moonlight. I dreaded snakes more than anything else that lives. I know now that it would not have harmed me.

"As it came out of the water and began to crawl through the reeds, I started up, and plunged blindly into the water to escape it. I made straight for the land, taking the bog as it came. It was a marvel that I got there alive. Perhaps my speed helped me. I ran so quickly over the surface that my feet had no time to sink. As I ran I remembered my father's words, and I made for the forest. No one stopped me: no one could have seen me, for no search was made. I have lived here in the trees ever since—I am very glad you have come."

Charlton was silent for a moment when the voice ceased, pondering over the strangeness of the tale; and it spoke again with a hesitation which it had not previously held. "But I don't expect you to believe me. You will have to see for yourself first; and then it may be too late to escape. I know it sounds an unlikely tale, and I haven't told you all, because I didn't want you to doubt."

The tone was almost plaintive now, and Charlton answered quickly "Oh, yes, I believe you. It's not the kind of tale that anyone would expect to be believed if it weren't true. Besides, I know it's true about the caves, and I've seen the satyrs. It's a bit stiff about the birds doing the garden, but, after all, elephants do similar work in India, so it's not very surprising.

"But there's one thing that puzzles me. Why didn't you go back to the cave to get the things you had left there? Clothes and things, you know. You must have needed them."

"I was afraid at first. I went to the further side of the forest and hid in the trees. I was afraid of being found. Afraid of the satyrs until I found they couldn't climb. Afraid of everything. Even afraid of the monkeys. Horribly afraid of snakes. That was my life. Just fear. There was plenty to eat. It was warm and dry. Gradually the fear left me. Then there came the noise of the next hunt, and I just lay and shook with fear in the fork of a great bough, a hundred feet from the ground. It was all fear, and a hopeless loneliness. But day by day I got more confident. There came a time when I ventured to cross the bog at a place which seemed safe, and began to search for the entrance to the cave, but I never found it. You see, there are miles and miles of the cliff-wall all covered equally by the great creeper, and I hadn't noticed carefully when I came out. It might take years of search to find it, and all the time there would have been the risk of being observed, and of being trapped in the caves if I should enter them. No, I was safer here. Don't you understand?"

There was an anxious note in the last question, for Charlton had fallen silent again, but from a different cause. A sudden doubt had disturbed him. Could he find the entrance to the cave? He thought he could, but he realised for the first time how small it was, and without outward sign in the monotony of the creepered wall. But he must face that stile when he reached it.

"Yes," he said, "I see. It must have been a terrible time for you, but we'll hope that it's over now."

Her heart quickened at the sound of sympathy and comradeship in his voice, coming after two years of isolation from her kind, during which it had been her habit to sit for hours in the high branches talking softly to herself, afraid that she should lose the power of speech if she should fail to use it.

"Can we hope to escape?" she said eagerly. "Will you tell me about yourself?"

"Well, I think we'll try," he answered with a new cheerfulness. He had been no less isolated than herself, though for a shorter time and with a different reaction. "If you can help me to handle a boat, we ought to be able to manage it. About myself? There's nothing really to tell."

But she pressed him, and he told her many things of his own life and of happenings in the world from which she had been divided, realising as he did so that she had the livelier interest in them. He had had life within his grasp, and had let it go indifferently past while she had hungered for it with a vivid vitality, thinking that she had lost it forever.

They talked, and the hours passed. They drew to a closer intimacy than might have come from months of more conventional acquaintance. Marcelle was hardly conscious of her nearer approach from the first cautious distance till he reached out an exploring hand, and a bare ankle was captured.

She thrilled to the touch with a sudden passion which alarmed and held her. Primal instincts warred with the controls and cautions of earlier years, and caught her breath as she called in protest: *"Oh, please—please—"*

There may be many men who would not have released her, if at all, for so light a pleading. There may be many women who would have been content to fall to such a capture, but a natural shyness, and a fastidious avoidance of the second-bests that life offers with such deceitful readiness, had left him with a virginity no less hesitant than her own, and with a respect for the integrity of womanhood which can only live under such conditions; he drew his hand back at once, and there was a pause of silence.

Then he resumed the conversation that his hand had broken. He had been telling her of the capacity of his boat, and they had been planning to escape together with the impersonal comradeship of a common need. It was the question of the nearest land of which he had been talking, on which she could give little help, for her geography was vague, and she had no knowledge of navigation. Neither of them had an exact knowledge of the position of the island itself. They agreed that it must be in the Eastern Pacific, a very spacious starting-point. He resumed now by suggesting that they should steer northeastward. Sooner or later, if they kept afloat, they must reach the American mainland. Before that, as he supposed, they would be likely to cross one of the great routes of ocean traffic, and would be unfortunate if they were not seen and rescued.

She agreed to this, but her voice was constrained with a new self-consciousness. He was aware that it came from a slightly increased distance.

There was a longer silence. "If there were any light!"—he thought; but the night was black in the forest. He remembered that he had never seen her face. What did he know of her, but the momentary twilight glimpse of a girl's back and the sound of a voice in the darkness? He remembered how he had more than once been roused to admiration of a woman's form, or a glory of hair, and then, when the head turned—he must wait till the light came. He could not believe that she would be less than adorable.

Marcelle also thought of the light, but with greater knowledge and a different purpose. She had not spent two years beneath the open skies without knowing when the moon would rise, and her alert watchfulness was already conscious of a faint change in the quality of the darkness which was her only clothing.

She had resolved to go before that change should come, and she was the more urgent to do so for the mental intimacy which had united them, and for the touch that had thrilled and warmed her. Also, she had a task to accomplish before the day came, of which she was afraid to think, though she was resolute to achieve it.

She spoke at last, trying to reach a casual tone, and conscious of a breathing which she controlled with difficulty. "I mustn't stay now, but I will come back in the morning, and we'll go and look at the boat, if you like, and then we can decide. There's no real hurry unless your shot was heard and they know you are in the forest, and that's not likely. But I shouldn't shoot again unless you must. And remember that the trees are always safest.

"Listen carefully to this. There's a tree on the further side of the pool, with low boughs and dark leaves, long and narrow. It's the only one of its kind just here, though they're common round the swampy places. It's quite easy to climb. There's a space where the branches spread out at the top of the trunk, where you can rest comfortably and would be safe forever. I'll come back about three hours before noon. Will you wait for me there? I shall come through the higher trees and drop down. If I don't come, you'll know that they've—that I can't—but I've no doubt I shall come."

"But why need you go? Why can't I come with you? Can't I help?" Charlton began, a score of questions and protests rising in his mind to delay her, but Marcelle had seen the dim outline of the tree beside her, and it was a high and distant voice that called farewell to his protests.

CHAPTER THIRTEEN

THE TUNIC

There was once a woman who started out to commit suicide, but observing a hole in one of her shoes, and having to pass along a street where she was known, on her way to the river, she returned to change them. After which she resumed her purpose.

Marcelle earnestly desired apparel before she should introduce herself in the daylight. It was about eighteen months since the last rag of the attractive garments in which she had landed had declined to identify itself with her further wanderings. Recalling the expedient of her first ancestor, she had endeavoured to provide herself with a covering of leaves. After some weeks of experiment, she remembered that Eve had received supernatural assistance, and she decided that it must have been needed.

Her efforts to manufacture garments for various parts of her person had succeeded in providing several which she could put on without catastrophe. Having assumed one of these, it remained in its intended position as long as she practised a similar immobility. When she moved, it could be relied upon to expose its own fragility and its owner's person.

If the second branch did not reproduce her original nudity, it was only because the first had relieved it of the opportunity.

After some weeks of these abortive experiments, she had desisted. While she had been engaged upon them, she had been able to look forward to a time when she would have resumed the symbols of respectability, as she had been taught to suppose them. By when she had abandoned her attempt, she had become accustomed to her appearance being as her Maker had (apparently) intended.

Probably there are women who would have been more persistent, more inventive, and more adroit in manipulation, but she had never been fond of sewing.

It is true that she had discovered a method of plaiting hats. It would have been more useful and more used—had she not been surrounded with such abundant shade. She need not ever feel the direct force of the sun unless she willed, and then she must climb to the highest boughs and find some airy perch where the light pierced the leaves of the crowding treetops.

Whether a hat can be considered a substantial reduction of a general nakedness is a point on which opinions might differ. It is important in churches. For a forest call upon a man whom she desired to impress favourably, Marcelle thought it inadequate. It was true that he had already observed her once without even so slight a tribute to the tyranny of civilisation. But that was involuntary, and the view had been brief and backward.

Marcelle recalled it, and her mind was untroubled. She was aware that she had a good figure. She smiled to herself. I think she dimpled, but this will never be entirely certain, for there was no moon. There will be those of her own sex to call her an abandoned woman. Women abandon each other so easily. But Marcelle smiled in the night.

Yet she had no mind to repeat such an experience. She had seen a man she desired, and she had a serene and youthful confidence that he was hers when she would. She had lived for two years the natural and primitive life of the tropic forest, but behind those years were all the experiences, the acquired instincts, the inhibitions of civilisation. Beneath all of the perversities of her mind, she knew that she regarded him as hers already. Rather, she intended that he should take her. Yet she was setting out at a desperate risk to acquire the means of concealing herself from him. She could not endure the damaged shoe.

Yet she thought that she might be losing all on the venture, and she crossed herself as she thought it. She had a faith of the kind which is difficult of comprehension to the Protestant or Agnostic temperament. A faith implicit and childlike in which fundamental verities were blended with myth and legend into an inexplicable and indivisible amity. It was not an exacting faith, for all its loyal sincerity. It was not entirely free from an unconscious impression that the obligation was mutual especially since it had become comparatively unpopular. Sins were to be avoided, but it was clearly understood on both sides that they were to be committed at intervals, and then confessed and forgiven.

It is true that there were essential rituals, which Marcelle was unable to practise, but that was not her fault at the moment. She had not, perhaps, been very regular in that direction when opportunities had been ample, but she had a happy confidence that *le Bon Dieu* was not inexorable, particularly towards young ladies of attractive appearance. And there was always His Mother. It has been well said that the great defect of Protestant Christianity is the lack of a female deity.

Marcelle crossed herself, and felt braver. God would not let her fall into the hands of those whom she was setting out to plunder. (It was a point of ethics which she did not pause to consider. The creatures whom she was proposing to rob were too far apart for any thought of mutual obligation to enter.) Nor did she doubt that she was doing rightly in risking life itself for the apparel she sought. To her mind there was no alternative possible, and what we must, we may.

She was of a fine courage, for she went on coolly and with a wise discretion, although she was desperately frightened.

She had no doubt that she could pass the palisade, though the hooved satyrs were unable. But she did not know with exactness what might be at any point upon the further side. She knew of more than one place where the trees grew close and high, and mingled with those beyond—places where the little monkeys crossed with impunity. She marshalled every scrap of memory regarding the position of woods and gardens; adding everything that the distant observations of the last two years had taught her. She thought of the wide gate in the palisade through which they entered the forest when they came to hunt the satyrs. There was a path from there that led, broad and straight, to the centre of the settlement. She had not passed along it, but she knew it at either end. The trees ran along one side of it for some distance from the forest. Perhaps, most of the way. She decided upon that line of approach. When the trees failed, she would take the path. She would make the quicker progress in the darkness, and the path would be almost certainly deserted. She must risk that, and trust to speed for her escape, if she should be seen. The real risk would come later.

As she planned, she did. The moon had risen now, and was sufficient to guide her. She would have asked for less light, had the choice been hers. She crossed above the barrier without difficulty, and continued for nearly a mile, passing from tree to tree beside the moonlit path. It would have been easier to descend and walk along it, but there was a feeling of security in her accustomed trees which she would not willingly lose. The path was empty of life. The movements that she heard around and beneath her were only such as were common to the tropic night. They held no threat of danger, but rather an assurance of security. They told of myriad activities that would have sunk into an instant silence had any voice or sound of distant step disturbed them.

But they did not cease as she passed, for she was free of the forest, and danger did not come from the high branches in which she lived.

So far, the little monkey that she had tended had followed, its agility and untroubled leaps through empty air enabling it to follow her longer reach and almost equal tree-craft.

Still she went on, and the moon rose higher and the path was vacant, though a yellow owl came drifting, silent as a dead leaf, along the airway above it.

Then there came a tiny sound from the monkey, and the girl paused in an instant, for she knew the danger-word of its kind which would pass, low as a movement of leaves, from end to end of the forest.

She became aware of some large shadowy shapes among the branches before her. Marcelle's heart beat fast as she saw them. She guessed at once that they were the great birds which the older community kept for their gardening. She had never thought of them as flying. Probably they ascended branch by branch, as a fowl will gain the higher perch of the poultry-house. But here they were, a hundred feet from the ground. She was afraid to go forward.

She moved, and they gave their first sign of having observed her. A hoarse squawking noise broke out. It was taken up by birds further away. It seemed that scores of these creatures must be perched in the trees before her.

She had no defence, should they attack her. She remembered their great beaks; their heads, which were higher than hers; and the sardonic intelligence of the eyes that had surveyed her as she had walked in the gardens. She had always dreaded them. Certainly she could not bring herself to venture among them. And there was a new danger in the noise which they were making. It might raise an alarm which would be fatal. And the time was passing.

She could not attempt another way through the trees, for they only grew thickly in a narrow belt along the roadside. There were trees on all sides, but they were separated too widely for any continued progress among them.

She must descend and take to the ground.

As she decided this, the little monkey called from below her. Fifty feet down, she found that the way was clear. The birds were only perched among the higher branches. She went forward quietly, though with an added caution. The squawking voices had stilled, as she left the higher level.

The trees grew smaller, and then ceased. Marcelle stood on the moonlit road. She was afraid to go on, dreading the peril of the adventure, and feeling a disconcerting sense of bareness, such as she had never known in the green depths of the forest.

There was little cover before her. To the right the ground rose park-like and undulating, colourless in the moonlight, but Marcelle knew it to be gay with the tamed luxuriance of a million flowers. Beyond was the dark mass of the temple, and the houses of the priests and their familiars. Before her, on the hilltop, rose the white feast-house, and to the left a bush-clad slope that fell away to the bog-land. She remembered the bushes, with their great blooms of tiger-yellow, shaped like a slender trumpet, that lifted sunward when the light called, and then declined again as the evening shadowed. Beyond these bushes were the white men's houses.

She had been uncertain whether to attempt her purpose there or at the dwellings of the older people, but the bushes decided her. She could crawl through them unnoticed. Also, she was more doubtful of the habits of the dark-skinned women. She did not know how or where they slept, or—in fact, anything. She knew nothing of their habits, nor had she entered their quarters.

She turned to the left.

Crawling through the bushes was possible. So far, she had been right, but it was neither pleasant nor speedy. It was necessary to lie low—very low at times. Necessary to wriggle flatly along ground that was stony in some places, and at others consisted of a damp adhesive clay with rough-barked leafless under-boughs scraping the back—boughs with an occasional projecting spike that gave a sharp penalty for too impetuous progress. It was hard, slow, uncomfortable work, and, worse than that, it was almost impossible to continue in a straight course in the root-impeded darkness. There was a heavy poisonous odour from the over-closing bushes, which made breathing difficult and the brain rebellious.

Having wasted half an hour, and made less progress than she could have done in five minutes on the open way, Marcelle gave up the attempt. She realised that time was passing inexorably, and that it threatened a greater danger than was probable from the open path in the night-time.

Standing erect once more, with trodden ground beneath her, she saw how high the moon stood, and calculated that the dawn was not more than two hours away. Men do not lie asleep after dawn in latitudes where day and night are equal, and noon is sultry.

She had a cowardly impulse to turn back, and to come earlier and more swiftly on another night, aided by what she had learned already. Perhaps it was no more than prudence that urged her, but, because she was in a panic of fear, she felt it to be cowardice, and refused the thought. She went on more rapidly. She passed Jacob

Sparrow's house, with its long verandas. It was built of timber, heavy and solid, different from the others. Demers' house was further on the left, and a score of others were beyond it. Would the moon give no shadow, just where it was most needed? On the darker side of a creepered porch she crouched and doubted. They were all around her now, and if one should call, she would be surrounded in a moment. Most of the houses were built of lattice work, the road being visible to anyone who might lie wakeful within them. Nothing stirred. There was no sense in this. Having come so far, she only increased her risk while she waited. With the sudden courage of desperation she made straight for the structure where the goat-foot servants slept who were neither women nor satyrs. It was thickly thatched, for rains were sometimes heavy, and the roof spread out and downward beyond the walls. It was walled halfway up, but less strongly, for winds were rarely violent, and the position was sheltered by the outer circle of cliff, and by the hill behind it. The upper halves of the sides were entirely open, except for the pillars which sustained the roof. Internally, it was divided into two compartments; one was used for the weaving of cloth from hibiscus-fibre, in which these creatures were employed when their services were not otherwise needed; one was their sleeping-quarters. They could not get out when the door was shut, for they were unable to climb. The method of building gave protection both from sun and wind and rain, with the abundant ventilation which the heat required.

Fortunately, Marcelle remembered in which division the day's labour was carried on. That would surely be deserted now. She climbed the wooden wall with a silent agility which she would have thought impossible two years earlier, and dropped quickly to the floor.

It was darker here than on the moonlit turf outside. Though the upper parts of the side wall were left open, the projecting slant of the roof prevented any direct moonlight from entering. But there was a diffused light that was sufficient for her purpose when her eyes had adjusted themselves to its requirement.

The apartment in which she stood was long and rather narrow, with looms and spinning-wheels ranged along its outer wall, and a row of benches before them.

On the opposite wall, against which she stood, many garments were hung on wooden pegs; some new, some sent for repair. Marcelle could have taken an ample armful, and escaped as silently as she had come. None would have stayed her. Had she done so, she might have saved many lives and much trouble to herself and others. But Marcelle was modest. She would follow the mode. And her mode was of Paris, not of the descendants of half-bred Chilean women. Modestly (which has no relation to virtue) is a somewhat tyrannous mistress. Marcelle was sure that she must have clothes. She was (if possible) surer that she would never wear those which she now found before her.

Let us be fair to those clothes. The material was good, and they were well-woven. As to their designs, it is at least certain that Marcelle would have worn uglier; had she been satisfied that a thousand other Parisians, of a satisfactory social standing, were making a similar exhibition. But having no such assurance, her mind was repelled by an ugliness which had no licence.

Besides, they would not fit her. Most of the island women were short and very thickly made, as mongrel women of certain descents are apt to be. That was their misfortune. It was their fault that indolence and gluttony had united to add a covering of fat to their natural dimensions. Their clothes were designed accordingly.

The creatures that wove them—it is difficult to classify them accurately either as animals or human slaves—appeared to take pleasure in their work, and some of them were very skilful, but their skill was not wisely directed.

They produced garments in which irregularly-shaped patches of crude and violent colours blended discordantly, one into another, or they portrayed objects upon them.

They were mostly of an ample size, for the amenities of the climate had not inclined these women to a reduction of covering, such as might have been considered a likely consequence. Rather, the fact that the garments could be produced in greater abundance than they could be worn had incited a spirit of competition among them, in which each strove to wear more than her companions.

This account may be tedious, but it is necessary. It explains why half an hour passed before Marcelle emerged again in the moonlight.

She tried garment after garment, and discarded them with a visible shudder of disgust. She disliked the prospect of meeting Charlton in a state of nudity. Would it be better to meet him in a garment the arms of which were absurdly short, the material between them sagging loosely in front, and in the same condition behind, however tightly she should lace it? A garment very light and thin and finely woven, but of which it could only be hoped that the colours would look better in the sun—a hope for which a very sanguine mind would be needed—and with images woven upon it, so that it looked, at the best, like the walls of a children's nursery?

She was quite sure that she was not going to introduce herself to Charlton's notice in so absurd a drapery.

In the midst of this dilemma she became conscious that the ugliness of these garments was more easily visible than when she had commenced to inspect them. With a start of fear she realised that the day was coming. It was at the same moment that she came upon something which she might consider to be at least a possible covering. It was a man's tunic, such as were worn on their hunting expeditions, leaving the legs free below the knees. The tunic was of a silver-blue colour and was without embellishment, except that its edges were embroidered in a darker shade. Marcelle seized upon it with avidity. To live nudely among the green shadows of the forest had become habitual. To introduce herself in such an aspect to a man of her own kind had seemed impossible. Worse, a hundred times, would it have been to walk unclothed through the village in the eyes of day. At that moment she would have willingly assumed the ugliest garment from the heaps around her.

She had vaguely intended to acquire some variety of wardrobe on this pilfering expedition, but she had no longer thought for anything but escape, if time should still permit it. Already there were sounds of movement on the other side of the partition.

Less easily than she had come, for the loose tunic embarrassed her, she climbed the wooden wall and dropped into the shadow of the veranda.

It was lighter than she had supposed, and the need for flight was urgent. Dawn comes quickly in equatorial regions. She glanced right and left, and saw no movement; but eyes might soon be looking from a score of dwellings. They might be looking now. She remembered that she was at the further end of the settlement. The idea came that she might be wiser to leave it at that side, though it was furthest from the forest, and to return by making a circuit through the bushy slopes that lay between the settlement and the bog.

She passed round the veranda and found that the woods were not a hundred yards away. There was no reason why they should have been cleared for a greater distance. There was no cause for cultivating the ground while food was abundant without effort. There was no fear of enemies, such as would make the denseness of the woods a possible cover for attack.

Marcelle crossed the cleared space very quickly. She was confident that no one had seen her. She came to a narrow path that ran into the wood. She remembered having explored this with her father, followed by a watchful retinue. She remembered that it led only to a little pool at the edge of the bog lands. So it did then, but that was two years ago.

She went on with a sense of exaltation. She could scarcely restrain herself from singing. She had done that which she came to do, and she was escaping to safety. Before her was freedom—companionship—other things, of which she was glad, and shy to imagine.

She had acted prudently, and her memory had not betrayed her, yet she went forward gaily to her own undoing.

She came to a stump of a felled tree. Then to several on her left hand, at the side of the path. Then to a fallen tree which lay across it. She attempted to clear it, forgot the impediment of the short but unaccustomed skirt, and came down rather awkwardly. She was bruised, but her temper was unruffled. She was too light-hearted for such troubles to invade her serenity. If she considered the trees at all, they gave her no warning. If they wanted timber, they cut trees. That was natural. What of it?

Then she came in sight of a bungalow, large, newly built. She was close upon it at the first sight, and as she stopped abruptly, a woman came out, if such she could be called. She had one human foot, and one that was hoofed like a satyr.

A tall and leafy tree was overhead, and with an instinctive resort to her accustomed safety, Marcelle reached for its lowest branch. She drew herself up, confident that she had escaped unnoticed.

Climbing higher, she observed that the tree in which she had taken refuge was isolated on three sides by the felling which had taken place around it. On the fourth another tree of a like kind grew closely, toward which she made her way, and then hesitated, for it had commenced to sway in an unnatural manner. She looked down through the leaves and saw that a man was moving below her. She saw also that there were ropes round the tree's trunk. She could not see from her position that it had been cut through most of its thickness, but the swaying motion, and a creaking, cracking sound from below were sufficient evidences of what was happening.

Could she cross it before it fell? It might be her one chance of safety. She was in the mood to venture, and knew that she was too late at the same moment. With a rending of strained boughs, and a final crack at its base, the wounded tree bowed over and crashed at an increasing speed through the surrounding branches of its neighbours that could delay, but had no strength, to support it.

Marcelle looked down, and became aware that the fall had exposed her to sight from below. She drew back hastily, and a man, who was already looking up to judge what damage the fallen giant had caused to the surrounding trees, observed her motion. Their eyes met with a mutual shock of recollection. It was Pierre, the carpenter.

CHAPTER FOURTEEN

THE CAPTURE

After the death of Marcelle's father and her own disappearance, there had been an hour during which Pierre's life had been somewhat precarious. M. Latour's revolver had been used to deadly effect; the girl was gone; there was no disposition to regard the introducer of these strangers with gratitude. The proposal that Pierre should be executed was popular, and only required the decision of Jacob Sparrow to have been carried out with a very cheerful alacrity. It was his craftsmanship that saved him, of which he had already given some demonstrations.

Jacob remarked very reasonably that he could use it to make any articles which were required, and that they could always put him to death if he should cease to be worth the keeping. As he proved useful, they kept him busy in their service. It was practical slavery, but was not onerous. As time passed, he was allowed to build a house for himself, but was directed to do this at some distance to the rear of the other dwellings. Later he was given a wife, but this was a woman who had been born with a single goat-like hoof, and who was regarded as only semi-human in consequence. There were cases of horns being more or less clearly developed which were accepted as of an admitted respectability. The fact that Jacob's son showed this feature so prominently was sufficient to protect it from any form of ostracism, but there had been no other case of a goat-foot child being born to a human mother. Had both feet shown this peculiarity, it is possible that the child would have been given to the companionship of the satyr-born slaves that were kept for cloth-weaving and various offices of domestic servitude. The difference between the two feet raised a problem which was adroitly solved by presenting their owner to the alien slave.

Pierre was a man of the blond French type, with a full, fleshy face and a beard that straggled widely, but had no density. He looked somewhat heavy and awkward in his build, but he trod with a silent lightness. His voice, like his tread, was very soft. He would have killed a sheep with tears in his eyes—and enjoyed the tears. He was a good workman, and industrious. He considered his own comfort, which inclined him to confine his more strenuous occupations to the coolness of the early morning hours.

There is no doubt that there had been a time, after their first landing on the island, when he had calculated that Marcelle was destined to become his personal property. He had despised Jean, and though he had not underestimated the character of her father, he had relied upon the absence of competition and his own attractions (which he may have overrated), even if the opportunity for more violent arguments might be deferred.

Marcelle had rejected his first advances with a contempt which she had been at no care to conceal, and this attitude had doubtless contributed to the complex motives under which he had betrayed her into the hands of the Sparrows.

She had shown her contempt, but there had been a secret fear which she had not shown, which came back as she gazed down upon him, joined with a rush of memories of those nightmare days of captivity, with the final scene of bloodshed and her father's death. She looked down, but she neither moved nor spoke.

Pierre was at least equally startled, but his mind adjusted itself the more easily. It was obvious that she had escaped the bog and remained concealed in the forest. For a moment he debated the possibility that she might have been kept in the settlement without his knowledge, but he rejected the supposition. The lives of the community were too open. Their houses were not adapted for such concealments. She might have been in the custody of the priest of Gîr, but the position in which he found her, and the pilfered garment, the significance of which he was quick to recognise, joined to other facts which his mind reviewed rapidly, made it improbable.

He realised what had happened very easily; it was less easy to decide on his own course of action. But he saw at once that he must first capture, and then conceal her, before the community should be astir. Then he would have time to consider. He supposed that Demers would have to have her. If only the old man were dead!

He addressed her in French, as casually as though it were a natural and expected meeting. "*Bonjour, mademoiselle*; hadn't you better come down and have some breakfast?" The question might have been humorous, or asked with a light goodwill, to relieve an awkward situation. But Pierre did not joke, and the soft tones were full of menace to the girl who heard them. She looked round, but the nearest tree was far beyond the possibility of reaching it. He noticed, and understood the glance; he saw that she made no movement to carry out his suggestion. He whistled to the woman who stood watching from the door of the bungalow, and gave her some directions which Marcelle could not hear, when she came to him. She went back into the hut.

He spoke again, as one who reasons quietly with a foolish child. "They will soon be about, and they will tear you to pieces if they catch you. You will be safe in my house."

She knew that she could very quickly be safer than in his house, if he would let her go, but she knew that he had no such intention. No less, she saw that she would gain nothing by remaining where she was. If she came down, she would gain nothing by having shown her reluctance. She dropped from branch to branch, very conscious of the impeding skirt, and feeling awkward in consequence, but to Pierre the revelation of her ease in the descent confirmed his first conclusion. He hated her because he knew that she despised him. There was nothing in common between them. But he desired her, as he watched her descent, with an animal cupidity, as he had done on the raft and in the cave, when he had lain scheming at night as to how at last he should get her.

His hand grasped her under the arm as she reached the ground. The woman had returned, and was holding out a short length of rope.

"Put your hands behind you," he said, "I shall have to tie them." She started at the word, and commenced to struggle furiously, but the grip of her arm held, though not easily. He was amazed at the strength of the little body that strained away from him. He had an impulse to put his strength into beating her to submission, but he answered, without raising his voice. "Don't be foolish. They would kill us both if they found us together, unless they thought that I had captured you for them. I shall only tie your hands. If you make a noise, they will be here in a moment."

She did not know why they would act differently because he had tied her hands, or what he meant, but she knew he was false, and she could not easily consent to such loss of freedom. But she had a great dread of those with whom she was threatened. She knew it was true that the noise of a struggle might bring them. Certainly true that he could call them at any moment, and hand her over to them if he would. She would have killed him gladly, as a quick glance told him. But then she relaxed, and answered in a voice which she tried to make casual. "Very well, if you think it's best; but don't do it too tightly."

She felt the brutal grip that bruised her arm slide down to her wrist. The next moment her hands were secured behind her in such a knot as a ship's carpenter would not be likely to fail to tie. They walked into the house.

CHAPTER FIFTEEN

THE TEMPLE OF GÎR

The priest of Gîr was alone with his wife in their private chamber at the rear of the temple. It was built, as was the temple itself, of blocks of hard red stone; square blocks each a cubic foot in bulk, and with surfaces that were smooth as glass. If any knew how or when they had been built thus, it was the old man who now bent over the table. But they showed no sign of age, nor did it seem that time had any power to destroy them.

Projecting ledges of stone, giving the effect of shelves along two sides of the room, were piled with papyri, containing the wisdom of a forgotten civilisation. In the centre was a table built of blocks of the same stone. It was constructed solidly, except that the stones were omitted at intervals to form kneeholes for those who might sit beside it. Blocks set into the floor before each of these kneeholes formed seats. Otherwise the chamber was bare, except that there was a pile of rugs in a corner, on which a child of about three years was sleeping.

The priest of Gîr was old, but of an undiminished vitality. Tall, lean, dark-skinned, handsome in a hawk-like way, with an air of authority which was habitual, he appeared to be equally incapable of human weakness, of human sympathy, or of human laughter. Yet his aspect was without baseness, as it was without generosity. It was austere and remote.

The chamber was lighted by a series of bracket lamps that showed the priest and his wife seated together and bending over a mirror which was laid flatly upon the table. As the light caught the surface, it showed now as water, and now as metal. The gazers were intent and silent, as though they saw something in its depth which was other than their own reflections. In fact, they saw the moon rise upon the path that led to the forest, and a figure that dropped from the trees and moved along it. They saw more than that. They saw into the coming days, and the part that they were destined to play in the tragedy which was now so closely upon them.

Suddenly the woman rose. "I can look no more!" she said in a tongue which was forgotten when the shepherd-kings were reigning in Egypt. "It is the end of all." She crossed the room and threw herself face downward beside the child. She made no further sound. The priest continued to gaze into the mirror.

At last he rose. He walked over to the woman.

"Urda," he said, "all is well."

"Well!" she cried. "And what of the child?"

"All is well," he repeated; "you should have looked longer."

"Need you do it?" she asked, after a pause of silence.

"No," he said slowly, "there is no need; but we have gone our own way twice before, and it has not proved a good one. It is the intended way that we see, and we can vary it at our peril. Had we not sought the easier path before, this would not be today."

"Yes," she said, "it is true."

They spoke no more, but went into the temple together. Husband and wife, brother and sister—their understanding was too close for many words to be needed. And the real tragedy was not in the events which had been foreshadowed. It was upon them already. Except for the sleeping child, they were the last of their race. Their son and daughter, husband and wife also, the parents of the child, lay dead together in the temple, waiting for the cremating pyre to consume them.

Eighty of their race there had always been till the strangers came. That was the ancient law. Every time that a child was born which would have increased their number, the community had voted, and the least efficient, or the least needed, the diseased, or infirm, or evil-minded man or woman or child, had been chosen for sacrifice. It was a good custom. It kept the standard of the race high.

They gave their blood to form the stones of which the temple was built, and their bodies to the fire. Every stone was coloured by the blood of the sacrificed, saved and included, how only the priests could tell, in those smooth red stones. The blood of many, beyond computing. It was a very ancient law.

But the two who lay dead before the altar now had not given their blood. They had not been chosen for sacrifice. They had died as none had been known to die—till the strangers came.

The strangers had brought disease. Strange disease, of which they had no knowledge, and for which they could find no remedy. It had seemed that all would die. And then the plague had stopped. But not entirely. Faster than their births, their deaths had been. And now the only two who could have continued the race lay dead together— and they had left but one child. It was the end.

The strangers did not know. They had never been allowed to know how fast the race had diminished. Looking in the mirror of fate, the priest had seen that they never would. That at least was sure, if he accepted the fate which the mirror showed. He looked up at the great temple-painting above the altar, which symbolised the enduring cry of mankind from their isolated planet to the Power which they feel but never reach, and through the desolation of his heart there came a thrill of exaltation. He saw that the end was the implicit sign of the eternal.

He must do the part that had been given him.

* * * * * * *

Urda had gone back to the sleeping child. She wished that she had looked longer, and had learned what its fate would be. Now she would never know. Even he who had seen could not help her here, for even between themselves such things might not be spoken.

CHAPTER SIXTEEN

THE HOME OF PIERRE

Marcelle was afraid and bitterly self-reproachful for the over-confidence which had placed her in such a needless peril. She sat on the wooden stool which Pierre had indicated for her use, and thought of the meeting with Charlton toward which she should now have been proceeding. She thought, with a maddening regret, of the free forest life which she might have lost forever. Yet the buoyancy of youth and health were still hers, and it was in no despairing mood that she considered the predicament into which she had fallen. Pierre did not speak. He sat with his eyes on the ground. He, too, was troubled by the uncertainty of the position, and unsure what the events of the day might be.

The woman fed Marcelle. There was nothing inhuman about her face. It was kind and sad, with a refined beauty. She might have sat for a Madonna. She was quiet, patient, alert to obey the will of her master even before it was spoken. She spoke little herself, and when she did so it was in French, which he must have taught her.

Marcelle decided that she was not unfriendly, but that there was nothing to hope for from that quarter. Nor anything to fear, unless it were from her obedience.

The room was airy and light, but less open to outside observation than was usual in the houses of the settlement. Yet Marcelle noticed that Pierre was watchful for any sound. Evidently, he did not wish her presence should be known, or at least not till his own time.

Could she not persuade him to let her go? She considered whether she should tell him anything of the boat, or of Charlton.

Why should they not take him with them? He would be an extra hand to help with the boat. Charlton had said that it was beyond his capacity. Pierre was a seaman, as well as a carpenter. It seemed a natural thing to propose that they should escape together.

But he would guess at once where the boat must be. Suppose he should leave her captive here and take it for his own use, leaving Charlton to his fate? She could not risk such a betrayal.

As she pondered thus, he raised his eyes, and looked at her speculatively. He commenced to speak, and fell again to silence. Then he rose. He looked at this wife. "You had better both stay here. Don't open to anyone till I return." He went out.

Marcelle felt the relief of his departure. Why should she not get up also, and walk out into freedom? She wondered whether she would encounter any active resistance from her companion, should she attempt it. But she quickly saw the folly of such an enterprise. With her hands so bound, what progress could she make? If she got the palisade unnoticed, she could not cross it. She must do better than that. Pierre's evident confidence that she was helpless was not encouraging. And he might return at any moment.

She considered whether there were any means of releasing her hands. She knew that a hero of romance would either work the rope loose, or rub it against some sharp object until it parted. Even were his feet bound also, he would contrive to roll into the required position. She felt that she ought to reach this standard of accomplishment, but there were difficulties. Her wrists ached horribly, even without straining them apart, and the rope showed no signs of relaxing. She remembered Pierre's knots, and the memory discouraged further efforts. The alternative method offered two difficulties. Pierre's wife was present and might interfere. More seriously, the sharp objects were not in evidence. The room held little beside a wooden table; some stools, such as that on which she sat; some deck-chairs, the seats of which were a net of strings woven from hibiscus-fibre; and a hammock of the same material slung from the roof.

Being a carpenter, Pierre must have had tools, but they were not in this room.

Marcelle watched the woman as she busied herself in such light tasks as the morning brought. She did not look unhappy as she moved about with an unconscious halting motion which probably arouse from the fact that her legs were of slightly different length, for she used either foot alone with an equal freedom. Nor did she appear to be greatly interested in Marcelle, or in the fact of her capture. It may be that she had found peace from the disgrace of her deformity, and the persecution of her childhood, in a spiritual aloofness which had ceased to be greatly troubled or impressed by surrounding circumstance. But Marcelle knew instinctively that she would obey her husband's directions, and that it would be waste of effort to make any attempt to divert her allegiance from him. Yet she felt that she might use her wits here to some purpose. She had more faith in her diplomatic abilities than in the devices of romantic fiction.

She ventured a few indifferent remarks, to which she received replies that were polite, though they went no further. The woman—her name was Rela, the origin of which may have been from any time or language from Judea to Chile—had a voice that was low and very musical, so that the most commonplace word came like a caress to the one to whom it was offered.

Then Marcelle came to the point. She remarked on the unseemly size of the tunic that she was wearing. Could a smaller one be procured? Rela looked at it quietly, and agreed with a surprising readiness. Yes, she would do that.

She agreed so readily—indeed, so indifferently—that Marcelle wondered whether she had been understood. But the fact was that Rela had an influence with the slave-workers in the clothing-house which made it easy for her to render her guest or prisoner the service for which she asked.

She agreed at once, but made no motion to put her promise into operation. Marcelle thanked her, and asked when she could hope to have the needed garment—she did not minimise the ugliness, nor the inconvenience, of the one that she was wearing.

The woman replied that she could not leave the house in Pierre's absence, but that she would fetch it on his return. This was not exactly what Marcelle had hoped—though it was more than she could reasonably have expected. It had occurred to her that she could not make the exchange while her hands were tied, and that the woman might possibly consent to loose them for such a purpose, though she might refuse if she were asked without a natural occasion arising. If once she got them free, she was determined that they should not be tied again, if her strength could prevent it. To defer the opportunity might be to lose it, but on the other hand, Pierre might now be returning at any moment, and if the woman chose her own time it might be best in the end.

Marcelle's thoughts reverted to Charlton, waiting, she supposed, at the spot she had appointed. How long would he wait? If only she had had the sense to tell him where she was going! She did not doubt that he would attempt her rescue, if he should be aware of the peril in which she lay. And perhaps lose his own liberty or his life in the effort, she thought, with a renewed bitterness of regret at the folly through which she had been captured. At that moment she would have given all the clothes that the world's looms have woven to have been two miles away in the freedom of the forest trees.

But regret was useless. However much she might reproach herself for the danger into which she might draw him, the hope remained. It was more than a hope, it was conviction that he would seek her. If she could find no earlier way to freedom, she must play for time, and await his coming.

Rela, glancing at her unobserved, was inclined to a mild wonder, seeing the smile that was on her lips. But it faded as there came a sound of approaching footsteps, and the smooth voice of Pierre outside the door. He entered, with another man coming close behind him. Marcelle had a moment of panic, thinking that it was Demers—come, perhaps, to take forcible possession of the bride that had escaped him previously. It was almost a relief when she saw the form of Jacob Sparrow, leaning on a heavy stick, and coming slowly through the doorway.

CHAPTER SEVENTEEN

JACOB AND MARCELLE

When Pierre had gone out, his resolution had been taken definitely, with whatever reluctance, to see Jacob Sparrow and inform him of the capture which he had made, rather than to take the risk of concealment.

He went straight to the home of the aged ruler of the community, and found him sitting on the veranda enjoying the coolness of the early morning. It was there that he spent most of his time, only removing to the inner side of the door during the heat of the day. The position was of some strategic importance, because his home contained the residue of the stores which his father had brought to the island a generation before, some of which, including the ammunition and an unexhausted variety of tools and implements, were irreplaceable from the island resources. This was the only residence which was solidly constructed and capable of being strongly secured. When Jacob left it, which was seldom, except for the periodic feasts (when the whole population would be under his eye, or their absence known and permitted), it was always locked and left in charge of certain trusted servants whose loyalty was secured by the privileges which they enjoyed, and which his death would very probably terminate. The temptation to attempt pilfering was also lessened by the difficulty of subsequent concealment in the midst of a community which lived so openly, and whose concerns and occupations were matters of common knowledge and continual gossip.

Jacob dozed at his door and surveyed the carpenter's approach through half-opened eyes, in which there was no friendliness, though the dull indifference of their glance gave no indication of the alert and cautious mind which was in ambush behind them.

Pierre was under no delusion as to the old man's feeling toward himself, though he would have been startled had he known how entirely his own purposes were read; or the definite plan for his destruction which was only delayed from week to week, that the community might not be deprived of his services till it should be considered necessary to remove him.

Pierre gave his skill to his masters' use with a suave and deferential manner that attempted no familiarity, and made no friendships. He waited for the old man's death. He saw that he could do nothing while he lived, but he was confident that he could find occasion to outwit his son, whose brutalities were only formidable the while his father's brains were behind them. Meanwhile he was too cunning to draw suspicion upon himself by any premature intrigue, or attempted confidence. He kept his thoughts to himself, the while he watched the differences and weighed the characters of those whom he served with so humble an alacrity.

But the old man, watching with a like intentness, and brooding over all he saw with a very ample leisure, had recognised him as a potential danger to his son's security, and he had made plans for his removal, which he delayed from time to time, as a man may delay the execution of the will on which may depend the peace and security of those who are dearest to him. There was still useful work for Pierre to do, and Jacob did not regard his own decease as an imminent contingency. So the days passed.

Facing the old man in the porch, Pierre came to the point at once. It would be obscure and tiresome to reproduce the debased and mongrel dialect in which they conversed. In substance Pierre said simply: "The girl was not drowned in the bog. She has been hiding in the forest. I have caught her among the trees I was felling."

Jacob took the news without visible emotion, though it must have been somewhat surprising. After a moment's pause, he replied: "How did you find her? It is easy for those who know to find."

Pierre could not mistake the accusation. It was not entirely unreasonable. It was singular that he, who had brought her to the settlement before, should now be the one to find her. The imputation that he had known more than he had told before would not be easy to meet. But he only answered, in a voice that was even smoother and more deferential than usual: "She was up a tree where I was felling. I think she had ventured there to steal clothes, which she had come to need. I have her in my house. I thought I ought to ask first what you wish."

Jacob was silent for a time. He considered Pierre, but he asked no further question. Then he rose slowly, leaning on his stick. He said: "I will see her. You had better come with me." He called to those within to close the house till his return.

He walked slowly down the centre of the path, where the light was strongest. He knew that he was going blind, and he was careful not to show his infirmity. He could still see clearly for a short distance. He seldom went abroad except to the feast-house, and he could have walked there in the dark. It was a road that he had known from childhood.

His going to Pierre's house would have attracted attention at another time, but this was the day of the monthly hunt, and the inhabitants of the village were already assembling at the other end, which was the nearer to the forest.

He walked painfully, dragging one foot. Slowly as he moved, Pierre kept a pace behind, not venturing to walk beside him.

He made no further allusion to Marcelle, but asked some questions regarding the fallen timber as he passed it, and the work on which Pierre was occupied.

Having entered the house, he stood looking at Marcelle for a moment. He was never quick to speak. He looked at Pierre and his wife. "Go outside," he said, "and do not listen."

When they were gone, he sat down on a stool opposite to Marcelle. He sat down awkwardly, and as though the operation of rising might not be easy.

Marcelle looked at him, and was not afraid. Woman-like, she was impressed by his age and infirmity, and she underrated her danger. She had a girl's confidence in her power to win her way with an old man, either by wit or cajolery. Gross as he was, he did not excite the physical repulsion which she felt toward his son, possibly because he did not threaten her integrity in the same way.

The old man questioned her directly. "Where have you been these two years?"

She answered simply: "I have lived in the trees," and then with a woman's inconsequence: "My hands are hurting me. I do not like them being tied."

He said: "That was Pierre's doing. He is a fool." But he did not propose to loosen them. He said. "Why did you come here?"

"Because I needed clothes," she answered. The truth was obvious.

There was silence after that for some time. Jacob Sparrow looked at her, and he resolved that she should be his son's wife, whether she willed or no. Physically, she was of a different order from the diseased and degenerate women of the settlement. In mind and character he was disposed to think her superior. With such a wife his son's position would be secured—and with Pierre's removal.

His next question came to the point. "You were to have married my son. Why did you go?"

She said. "It was when they started to kill Jean. I was frightened. And then you killed my father among you."

It was plausible, but not convincing. Jacob did not doubt that she would escape again if she could. Marcelle saw clearly that she must persuade him of her willingness for the marriage, if she were to have any chance of freedom.

He said suddenly, "Do you like Pierre?"

The question surprised her, but the start of repulsion with which she met the suggestion was unmistakable in its sincerity.

Jacob spoke deliberately: "You cannot escape from the island. Do you not wish to marry?"

"Yes," she said. "I might." A thought which he could not follow dimpled her cheek as she answered.

He continued. "If you wish to marry, you must prefer the best man you can get. My son will succeed me. He will have everything. He is the best man here. There is no other so tall, so strong, or so brave as he. You shall be the first of his wives. You shall be the only one, if you wish, and if you will bear him sons. Are you not willing to have him?"

Marcelle was silent. She felt that a ready lie might give her the opportunity of freedom, but it would not come. She loathed Demers too utterly. The most that she could do in the cause of duplicity was to look down with an expression which was only faintly troubled.

Jacob put his question again, but in other words: "Are you not content to marry the best man in the island?"

She looked up, and her face changed. "Yes," she said, and there was a note of unmistakable sincerity which he had heard when she repudiated any liking for Pierre.

Magna est ventas. Even to deceive, truth is more powerful than falsehood. It did not occur to him that there might be another man on the island whom she would prefer to Demers. How should it? He was very sure that the priest of Gîr would not look at any woman but his own wife, and his age and aloofness made it an improbability that he would be in her thoughts. She had shown her feeling toward Pierre. So far his judgement was right. She might have seen from her leafy ambush some other man of the community who had attracted her fancy, but it was not probable. He had spoken truly when he said that his son was the strongest and the most courageous. He reflected that the position was different from when her father was living. She had had two years of solitude. After that (he supposed) there were few men that a girl would not be glad to take. And there was the fact that she had come into their midst from the security of her hiding-place, with whatever excuse for her temerity. On the whole, he was satisfied that his son was her choice. Besides, did it matter? If Demers wanted her, he would have her. There was no other man that would question his claim, or thank her for bringing him into such a quarrel. Jacob was sure of that.

On the whole he was satisfied beyond his expectation. He intended that Demers should have her, and he would have been quite content for his son to have beaten her into submission, but if she were willing, he was the better pleased.

He said: "You shall see him in the evening. He is hunting today." He rose slowly as he spoke.

Marcelle smiled in reply. He could not doubt that she was pleased at the result of the interview. So she was. He could not know that it was the ease with which she had deceived him, or rather that he had deceived himself, and the fact that Demers was away in the forest, that made her eyes alight, and gave a new hope to her heart.

She said: "My hands hurt me," and looked at him as though relying upon his assistance to release them.

He said: "We will soon alter that. Come with me." He went toward the door.

She rose and followed, though doubtfully. Pierre and his wife stood under the trees about ten yards away, waiting permission to return to their dwelling. Jacob led the way along the path without giving them any notice.

The sight of Rela recalled the promise she had made. Marcelle stopped, and gave Jacob a glance that was at once confident and appealing. "Rela promised to get me some better clothes," she said.

Jacob paused, in his usual manner, while he considered the implication of this statement. "You must come with me now," he said. "You shall have all the clothes you want."

Marcelle saw that she could gain no more for the moment. Evidently he did not intend to release her hands. She walked on beside him, looking demurely submissive, and accommodating her freer stride to his dragging steps.

As they were going Pierre followed, and caught them. He stood in the path with an expression submissive and yet resolved. He was a head taller than Jacob, and in every way the larger man: but with his head bent, he looked something like a revolting sheep or perhaps not a sheep, but in sheep's clothing only.

"I shall have the reward?" he asked, in the low suave voice that seemed to apologise for its own existence.

He waited anxiously through the usual interval of silence. He expected refusal. He knew that Jacob loved his gold, and the promise was two years old and made under different circumstances.

Jacob looked at him coldly, but the answer, when it came, was unexpectedly complacent. "You shall have the reward. At the wedding—tomorrow night. Yes—you shall have the reward."

The words were all that could be wished. The tone was quiet and expressionless. But Marcelle, her hearing trained to the interpretation of the faintest sounds of the forest life which she had made her own, thought that there was something ironic that underlay it; something of menace, that was not in the words, but in the thought that lay behind them. Pierre stepped back with an expression of gratitude and humility, but Marcelle shivered in the sunlight.

In Jacob's mind a thought that had come to him many times as he sat at the head of the feast-day board and watched the carpenter at the lower end, his broad hunched shoulders appearing apologetic of his own existence, took shape and resolution the while the question had been asked and answered. Yes, it would be sooner than he had intended. And simpler also. He should have his reward.

CHAPTER EIGHTEEN

THE HOUSE OF JACOB

Jacob's house was different from the others around it: the main portion, in which his goods were stored, was built of timber, heavy and strong, and roofed in the same material. But around this central solidity there were a number of rooms more lightly built, and differing little in structure from the prevalent style of architecture, except that the roofs were wooden (Jacob thinking that the usual thatch would add to the danger of fire, which was a constant dread to his mind) and that the door was stoutly made and strongly fastened.

His servants, watching through the latticed walls, saw his approach, and the door opened without knocking. He went in, and Marcelle followed. He led the way along a passage which ran along the side of the outer wall. This wall was lightly built, with a broad strip of lattice continuing along it, at a convenient height for observation by those within. Some light came through, but it gave an effect of darkness to anyone passing from the strong sunshine without. Marcelle noticed little till she had been led into a room which opened from the inner side of the passage. It had no door, but a wide aperture only. Through this, some light entered from the passage. There was no window. Like all the rooms, similarly ranged round the central store, it had no means of exit except by the outer passage.

Having entered here, Jacob turned to Marcelle, and stood facing her in an impassive silence, as his habit was before speaking to any serious purpose. It would have been disconcerting to a nervous temperament, but the girl had the advantage of a physical condition that required a more definite cause to perturb it. During the silence of the walk, the thoughts of both had been active, and Marcelle was now resolute to deceive him into such a confidence as would give her the opportunity of escape for which she was watching. She had seen clearly that her knowledge of Charlton's presence, and of the boat by which they might escape, was a concealed factor which might easily upset his most logical calculations. She saw that she had a perilous battle to fight, but, if she fought it well, she had some confidence in an ultimate victory.

Jacob weighed her words, and estimated her position shrewdly enough, so far as his information went, and he judged that she would submit to his will, but he was not quite sure, and the doubt angered him. He felt instinctively that there was some important fact that he did not know, though he could not imagine what it could be.

He spoke slowly and impressively, leaning forward as he did so with both hands on the heavy stick, for he rarely stood for so long a time, and the weight of the gross body tired him. "I will send someone to untie your hands. They will bring you food, and all the clothes you wish. I shall give you to Demers tomorrow night, telling them all what your position will be. You will go home with him when the feast is over, or when you have drunk sufficient. He has three wives. You can turn them out, if you will, and I will give them to others. But you will be foolish if you do. You will be the first in the island. The priest of Gîr is nothing, nor are his people, whom we never see."

He was silent for a moment, and went on in a different tone. "I don't think you will try to deceive me again. But if you do—" His voice changed again, he thrust his head forward, he took a step nearer to the girl who stood facing him, her hands fastened behind her, but who held her ground and returned his look without flinching. "If you do, understand that I will catch you, though I fell every tree in the forest, though I burn it down, though I clear it of all the food it contains. I will let them hunt you as they hunt the satyrs—*and for the same fate.*"

She faced this sudden burst of passion with at least an outward courage. She was cool enough to wonder whether it were genuine, or nothing more than an attempt to scare her.

She said, in as light a tone as she could command: "It doesn't matter, because it won't happen. I shouldn't like to be hunted like that. But I didn't know you were cannibals."

Jacobs laughed in derision. "Do you think they wouldn't be glad of the change? We have eaten satyrs once a month for fifty years. Do you think they would mind the change, if I set them on you? Just try, and you will get no mercy from me. Have you seen them killed?" He went out.

He was satisfied that she would make no attempt to escape after that. If she had had a doubt in her mind before, he did not think she would dare to do it, after the warning he had given her. But he took no risks. He gave such orders as the occasion required, and he resumed his seat in the only doorway that the building possessed.

His servants came and untied her hands. They brought her food in plenty. They brought her clothes from which to choose, only protesting, when she asked for a shorter tunic similar to the one she had, that it was not a woman's garment. She replied that it would be when she had worn it, and had her way. She supposed that the chief wife of Demers could set any fashion that she would. For the moment she almost brought her acting to the point of reality.

But she got a tunic of the length she wished, short enough to leave her the free use of her limbs, and of a single colour. They brought her sandals of satyr-skin, which she put on without enthusiasm, for her soles were of a polished hardness which was little likely to suffer from the floors or paths of the settlement.

Having supplied her needs, they left her to her own devices. The heat of the day was approaching, and in spite of all the excitement and anxiety of her position she was conscious of the need for sleep. She had not rested at all during the previous night. A very comfortable hammock invited her occupation.

Entering it, she fell asleep almost immediately, but the afternoon was not far advanced when she found herself awake again. It is said that sleep brings counsel and courage. To Marcelle it did neither. She had fallen asleep afraid, but yet confident that she would escape the danger that threatened her. It had not seemed very imminent. There was till tomorrow night in which to escape. Once in the forest, the way of freedom was before her. A way which they could not guess. And any moment Charlton might come to her rescue. Besides, she was very tired. It was pleasant to think that she might sleep, and he might be on his way to her assistance the while. She had an unreasoning confidence both in his will and in his power to release her.

But she woke in a different mood. The room was hot and oppressive. It was not usual to use these ill-ventilated apartments in the heat of the day, except in the time of rains. To Marcelle, after two years beneath the open sky, it was an intolerable oppression.

Her wrists hurt her acutely—more than she had realised when she had been physically tired. There were deep weals round them where the cord had cut.

When she slept, the crisis had seemed distant—tomorrow night, at the worst. Much might happen in the meantime. Many chances might aid her. She woke to the memory that Demers was returning from the hunt, and that the day was passing. Any moment he might enter upon her. How should she meet him?

Two years ago he had been ugly, brutal, uncouth, a repulsive savage, but he had been visibly uncomfortable beneath her father's critical eyes. Till the hour of the expected wedding he had not attempted any familiarity. Her father had always been beside her. He had not doubted that she would be his for the three days' waiting.

But he was then an overgrown youth of sixteen years—years of the quick growth of tropic climates. That was two years ago.

Could she manage him now, even for an hour? Could she conceal the loathing that made her sick at the thought of any physical contact? Could she deceive him as—she hoped—she had deceived his father? Had she even succeeded in deceiving him? She remembered the question with which he had left her. *"Have you seen them killed?"* She had. It was not a pleasant thought. Suppose she were consigned to such a fate at once, if she should show her real feelings! She knew how they would enjoy being let loose on her. She imagined their knives. She had a vivid imagination—and she had seen the slaughtering of the satyrs. To be hand-led and tortured for their amusement—to be bled and skinned—to be cooked and eaten.

Was it so much better than to resign herself to the safety of the road that opened before her? "The things we would not, those we do." It is true of all men, but of none so much as of those of mixed nationality. Marcelle had inherited the beauty of her mother's race, and the charm and personality which is more than beauty had been the gift of her father's parentage. In the same way the ideality which is at once the strength and weakness of the English character was confused by the vein of hardness which is in all the Latin races, and by the faculty of logical thought, which gains in clearness what it may lack in depth, and is at least free from the vice of evading its own conclusions.

Her reason told her that it was improbable that Charlton would come to her rescue. He was little more than a stranger. He had not seen her face. He did not know where she was.

If he came, what could he do? Was it not the only sensible course to accept the position which offered? What was Demers but a loutish youth that any woman could manage? Searching for any avenue of escape from the fear that was upon her, her mind went further. If she were forced to marry Demers, need it be a lasting bondage? There could still be Charlton in the woods—and a boat in the cave. Even Charlton would understand and forgive her, acting under such compulsion. Besides, he had no claim upon her. What would there be to forgive? He would not want to live all his days alone in the wood. He could not go, for he could not handle the boat alone. Oh, yes, he would forgive her very easily! Marcelle dimpled at the thought, as she had once smiled in the night.

But she did not want to do it—there might be still time—there might still be a way. Her mind went back to the woods. How she wished that she had never come!—and that she had not lingered! Even the choice of clothes that had hindered her was clear to her now in its essential triviality. Surely he would seek her when she did not return. Suddenly she burst into a passion of tears. She had not known a tear for two years—since those first weeks of fear and loneliness, and grief for her father's death. But now she cried—and cried; *"Oh, Charlton, Charlton, come quickly!"*

But Charlton was not coming.

After a time she heard voices and the sound of steps outside the house. She went into the passage, and looked out through the lattice. There she saw the man she most dreaded. Demers came to his father's door. Behind him were those who carried the spoil of the day's hunting.

As she looked, her face changed. *"I never will,"* she said, *"never!"* As she spoke she heard a movement. She turned, and saw an old woman standing beside her. She was much older than Jacob. Wrinkled like a dried fig. So small and bent that she was scarcely higher than Marcelle's elbow. Her eyes were small and black, and full of an alert suspicion. Fortunately, Marcelle had spoken in her father's language.

She went back into the room, tearless and resolute. She did not know what had made her decision so clear and so final. She had often seen Demers before. He did not look in any way worse than usual. But she knew that the thoughts of fear, or compromise, or surrender, were put aside, and that she had resolved to fight it out to the last.

Would she have had such courage if she had never met Charlton if she had been so caught with no alternative, and with no hope of ultimate escape or rescue? It is her sufficient honour that she was equal to the test to which her fate, or perhaps we should say her own folly, had brought her.

Demers spoke with his father in the porch, but he did not enter. Apparently Jacob had decided that they should not meet till the next day.

Marcelle went back to the hammock. No one disturbed her. She lay still, and at times she heard stealthy movements, as though someone were alert in the passage. She lay awake for a long time, full of anxious thought, but there were no tears now. She debated whether she should attempt escape in the night, but she doubted its wisdom. She felt sure that she was being watched, and an abortive attempt would be an added disaster. She decided that she must appear content, and watch for any circumstance that might befriend her.

So the night passed, and the morning followed—and Charlton did not come.

CHAPTER NINETEEN

THE HUNT

Charlton had lain awake for some time after Marcelle left him. Her tale was strange, but he knew it to be confirmed at every point where his own observations could test it. Anyway, he believed it. He was not in a mood for scepticism. He only longed for the return of one whom he might not know when he saw her. He loved a voice in the night.

Falling asleep, he did not wake till the sun had risen over the cliff-top, and a ray of light, slanting down where the pool made a break in the high canopy of the forest, touched his face, and its heat disturbed him.

He was first conscious that there were troubled noises in the air. The peace of yesterday had left the forest. Monkeys in the branches overhead chattered uneasily. Satyrs barked their warnings, now from one side, now from another. A louder, more distinct noise gained in volume, sounding like the advancing cries of a crowd, and then receded. He recalled that Marcelle had told him that this would be the day of the monthly hunting. He became conscious of the insecurity of his own position. The forest threatened, and his mind recalled the foreboding with which he had first beheld it, and the fear which had dominated him in the dream which had revealed it beforehand. Yet this feeling did not cause him to forget that Marcelle was to return, nor had it power to overcome the excitement of the anticipation. He recalled that she had directed him to the shelter of the tree which was their appointed meeting-place. He decided that it would be wisest to seek such security as it could offer, without waiting for the hour that she had appointed.

Making his way round the pool, he found it easily. It was not likely to be approached by any without a definite purpose, for the ground in which it grew was a deep mud, and on one side it over-hung the pool. It was not difficult to climb, and on reaching the top of the hole he found the place of concealment of which she had told him. Here he could lie flatly, and in some comfort, and observe something of the ground below, though not much. He had a clear view of the pool, and of the drinking-place on the opposite side. Above his head the boughs of a greater tree extended far out over the water. Its leaves were a light and vivid green. It bore a profusion of small cream-coloured blossoms, with an orange centre, and having a delicious but intoxicating scent, so that, as the day advanced, he found it hard to retain a watchful consciousness.

The cries died in the distance. The forest recovered something of its former peace. The heat increased. The appointed hour was past. But Marcelle did not come. He supposed that in some way the hunt might have delayed her, though he could not imagine why. He did not doubt that she had intended to keep her promise, or that she would be able to do so. He was impatient rather than anxious.

Then the cries of the hunt rose again, returning from another direction. There were sounds of movement below him, at the edge of the pool. He looked down cautiously, and saw three satyrs, an adult pair and a half-grown female. The male had a damaged hoof, and moved slowly and as though in pain. They were conversing with low sounds which seemed scarcely articulate, but must have had meaning to them. He had a fancy that the female was urging something to which the male consented reluctantly. If so, she had her way, for he moved down to the edge of the pool and entered the water. He swam rather slowly across the pool—Charlton had not thought that satyrs could swim, though it was natural enough—but did not attempt to land on the further side. He chose a place where the bank sloped abruptly, and stood in deep water beneath a luxuriance of overhanging creepers, only his head appearing above the surface. The two others watched till he had done this, and then disappeared in the woods.

Turning his attention from this incident, Charlton became conscious that the noise of the hunt was much louder, and was approaching the further side of the pool.

It was not long before a satyr came running down the path to the drinking-place. He ran slowly, and was evidently exhausted. His hairy sides were matted with sweat, and there was a smear of blood on his left haunch where a pike had grazed it.

He had escaped for the moment, because powder was getting scarce, or so Jacob said—no one knowing the truth but he—and his orders were that the muskets were not to be used unless the noon should pass without a victim having been secured. This one, being almost cornered, had evaded his pursuers through his knowledge of the undergrowth, but he was being hotly chased, under the impression that he was more badly wounded than was actually the case.

Now they were close behind him. He plunged into the water, swimming straight for the spot over which Charlton was stationed. His hunters hesitated, and then commenced to circle the pool, some in their direction. There was no path, and their progress through the bushes was not rapid. They had the longer way to go. Had the satyr been fresh, he might have escaped, but he swam slowly. When he landed he was a few seconds ahead, but he was not many yards from the water when the giant form of Demers, who had outpaced his followers, burst through the bushes. He had a musket in his right hand, which he held halfway up the barrel, with the butt foremost. He drove the butt hard between the shoulders of the panting satyr, who staggered and fell face forward. Demers put a heavy foot on the fallen body, and gave a bellow of triumph which was echoed by his approaching companions.

It was echoed also by a party of hunters whom Charlton had not heard previously. They were approaching from the other side, in full chase of two young males that they had just beaten out of their cover. They knew the significance of Demers' shout, and slackened their pace at once. So also did the satyrs that they had pursued.

Demers had thrown down the musket. He had a long knife in his hand. He was on his knees beside the prey that he had run down. He had rolled the fallen body over, and several of his followers had come to his aid, grasping the limbs of a creature too overcome by exhaustion and terror to make any effectual resistance. The two satyrs that had been chased a moment before now crowded fearlessly up, knowing that more than one was never taken at these monthly chases. One of them, bending over Demers to see which of his companions had been taken, gave an audible chuckle of satisfaction. Demers heard the sound, and looked up. Turning suddenly, he caught the creature by one hoof, and jerked it off its feet. As if fell, he threw his weight upon it, shouting to his companions. "Let that one go. This is fatter."

The animal struggled furiously, almost getting clear for a moment, but there were a dozen of them upon him. He barked terrified protests. Demers used the knife to quieten him with a practised hand. The barking changed to a series of sobbing screams. The satyr that had been released so unexpectedly struggled to his feet. He seemed dazed, and walked unsteadily. He went into the bushes, not appearing to notice the crowd of men and satyrs that were collecting from all sides around the scene of the slaughter.

Charlton, looking aside from a scene that was not attractive to contemplate, noticed a form that still hid under the overhanging growth at the farther side of the pool. He wondered why it had not come out to join its fellows. Possibly it did not wish that the men should observe its hiding-place.

He made no further effort to penetrate the leafy screen that hid the scene of blood and tumult beneath him. He had seen enough. His wanderings had familiarised him with many primitive conditions of life, which he had accepted without any acute emotional reaction. They did not touch his own life, and the lethargy of illness had left him only superficially interested in the moving drama around him. But the spectacle of these degraded beings, who were not savage, but degenerated from his own civilisation, affected him differently, and he was in a physical condition that was more sensitive to its environment than he had been previously. It is doubtless true that the men and women that Captain Sparrow had landed upon the island had been subnormal, both in intellect and in moral stability. That is a reasonable supposition, considering their occupation and antecedents. The effects of indolence and self-indulgence, and the contamination of the creatures upon which they fed, had produced a second generation which were a burlesque of humanity. But it was a burlesque without humour. It was like a jest in hell.

And yet how deep was the real gulf between these people and the character of the race from which they sprang? An English woman will say that she could not bear to kill a sheep, or even to see it slaughtered, while she lifts the mutton to her mouth. She is not consciously hypocritical. Nor is there any real inconsistency between her words and her occupation. She is only mistaken in the supposition that she is moved by anything but an entire and complacent selfishness. Her objection is not that her presence would be detrimental to the sheep, but only that it would be unpleasant for herself.

"I grieve for you," the walrus said; "I deeply sympathise."

She is as sincere as was the carpenter's companion.

If the European must live on the flesh of his fellow creatures, it may be advantageous that he should enjoy slaughtering them. It increases the sum of the earth's pleasures, and does harm to none.

Having no sense of humour, a vegetarian once complained that he had been gored by a bull. That animal has the reputation of being somewhat stupid, but, had he known the zeal with which the vegetarian preached a doctrine which would have involved the comparative, if not absolute, destruction of his kind, it is not conceivable that he would have let him escape with some bruises and a broken rib.

The domestic animal is served from birth to death by those who will ultimately devour him. They build houses to shelter him. They toil to grow the foods which he prefers. They perform the most menial offices for his comfort. They are his servants in all things, and, did he not finally pay them the due wage of his carcass, they would not be servants, but slaves. If such creatures have a grievance, it is that man is the cause of their degeneration in character and intelligence, owing to the comfort and security in which they live.

This is logical enough; but if it occurred to Charlton at all (which is doubtful), it did nothing to alter the aversion which he had conceived for the creatures that were making merry beneath him. If there be anything which is more certainly wrong than a scientific fact, it is a logical argument. Yet we shall continue to be fascinated by the marvels of science, and to pursue the study of logic. In so doing we are at least on a higher plane than is the man who avoids the use of the split infinitive.

Charlton's feeling was that it would be intolerable to live in a place, however fertile or beautiful, which was so inhabited—intolerable, either to associate with them on whatever terms, or to remain permanently in their neighbourhood, even in concealment. As they were too numerous to be easily exterminated, his mind turned to the boat. But for one consideration, I think that he would have descended the tree when the silence told that they had departed, and made his way back to the cave, with the purpose of loading up and departing immediately to whatever fate the seas might offer. It was not that he was afraid. He was of a nature to which fear does not come easily, unless at an immediate urgency. But he felt as one who seeks escape from the foul air of a sewer. Yet he did not go, and, as he elected to remain, he realised the bondage into which he had fallen. He loved a voice in the night.

There was silence now on the blood-drenched ground. Only a distant and lessening murmur told where the disturbers of the forest peace were retiring in an excited hilarity. The trees woke to life. Parrots called and monkeys chattered. Charlton could hear the discordant cries of a hundred bright-plumed birds that have no use for song, because they do not woo by sound but by colour. The sun was past its midday height. She had said that she would come before noon. It could easily be supposed that she would fear to venture while the hunting rabble had been immediately beneath him. Perhaps she had been all the time in the high branches overhead. But why did she not come now?

No man (except he be very young) expects punctuality from a woman, unless he have experience of her individual capacity. Charlton did not expect it. He knew that clothes are more important than the passage of time, and that incalculable periods are occupied in their adjustment. He wondered whether the dress resources of his new acquaintance might be less than satisfactory, and she delayed while she improved them. This was true, as we know, beyond his wildest imagination. But as the day advanced, the reason became increasingly inadequate. As evening approached, he considered whether it were possible that he had mistaken the tree to which he had been directed, but a search of the surrounding forest convinced him that this was impossible.

He returned to the appointed spot, and waited there till the evening darkened. He had decided by then that, having been deterred by the alarm of the hunt from coming at the hour she had appointed, she had postponed her intention until the night. It seemed natural that she should visit him in the darkness. But he could not be sure whether she would expect to find him in the place where he had been sleeping during the previous night, or in that which she had appointed for the daylight meeting. He decided that she would be more likely to look for him on the ground, and that in any case she would seek him if she could not otherwise find him. So he descended, but not to sleep. For he was now restless and anxious. He lay awake, listening for a motion in the leaves above him, and for a voice that he did not hear. The night was cloudy over the forest, and oppressively hot. It was damp also, and at times a warm rain fell though little penetrated the thickness of the shade above him. He was impatient to hear her voice, and to urge her departure with him. He must rescue her from this—yes, Jean's had been the right words—from this island of devils. They would not wait a moment after the moon rose, and they could be well on their way to the caves before sunrise. Perhaps they might actually have reached them, if she were able to guide him sufficiently.

But the moon rose and she did not come, and impatience gave place to fear. It became too evident that some accident or misadventure had delayed her. Unless—but he would not think of it. He could not think she was false. And yet—he had told her so much. He had told her of all he had, and of where it could be found. And what was she but a voice out of the darkness? The worst of women might have a voice that would win confidence. Yet he would not think it. But it put a fresh fear in his mind, which would not quieten till he had decided to return to the caves in the morning, and satisfy himself that all was safe. Besides, what could he do? He could not seek her in the trees. He might make such a search for months in vain, unless she willed that he should find her. He would do even that, if there should be no other way. But first, he would return to the caves. If it were needful, he would seek her even in the abodes of the half-men that he had watched and loathed. He did not think that it would be necessary. Why should he? But some half-hearted words returned to his mind with a weight of foreboding that they had not borne at the time. Had she gone into some danger, necessary before she should leave the island with him, the nature of which he could not guess? The thought did not impress him as probable, yet it influenced his decision. If she did not come by sunrise he would go to the caves, supply himself with some extra cartridges and other things that he needed, and would then commence a cautious exploration of the inhabited portion of the island. Having resolved on this course, he slept at last, though very briefly, for it was within an hour of the dawn that woke him.

CHAPTER TWENTY

THE VENTURE

Looking back in the light of after-knowledge, Charlton was always disposed to blame himself for the time which was lost in his journey to the cliff-side. It seemed to him as though, while the woman that he loved was in peril, he had thought first of the safety of some tinned food.

He was at a loss to supply any adequate reason for the course he chose. Yet it was not really discreditable to himself, nor difficult of explanation.

He had no definite knowledge of Marcelle's peril, or of where he might find her; he had not intended to be away for more than a day when he set out, and he had no other home or place or security of any kind; he wanted various things, though (apart, perhaps, from the larger supply of cartridges), they were not of great importance. Finally, there was the doubt which had been in his mind since Marcelle had told him of her inability to find the entrance when she had attempted to return. If he were to have a similar difficulty he would prefer that it should be while he was free from pursuit or any imminent danger. He wished to be sure that this line of retreat would be open and could be rapidly taken; then he could give his mind to the finding of the girl with whom he wished to share it.

In fact, he found the entrance with little difficulty, though he was favoured in this both by good chance and by the careful survey which he had taken of the surrounding scenery in the days before he had ventured out.

He found everything as he had left it.

He felt the need for rest, which was natural after an almost sleepless night and the watchful tension of the previous day. He decided to remain in the security of his retreat till afternoon, when he would commence a systematic search for the girl whom he desired so much, and of whom he knew so little. His mind relieved by decision, he slept for several hours, waking abruptly to a dream of a voice that called him through the darkness of the forest night, not as he had heard it before, in friendliness or in laughter, but with a note of urgent fear.

He had been content before to go with his weapons loaded, and with a handful of additional cartridges in a jacket pocket; but now he increased the quantity. He also fetched out the sword which he had hidden behind the chest, and considered how best he could carry it. After one or two unsuccessful experiments he corded it over his left shoulder. It seemed a novel method to choose—he was not aware that the heavy two-handed swords of the Middle Ages were often carried in this position—but in the absence of belt or frog, he could not adjust it securely at his side, nor would he risk that it should impede his climbing. He did not burden himself with food, having learnt that it could be found in abundance on the forest boughs. With the rifle slung over his back, his hands were free. He broke away the creeper from the entrance sufficiently to be a guide to the approach as he would near it on his return, though not so that it could be seen too easily from below. On reaching the ground, he marked and memorised very carefully the place where his return ascent should be recommenced. How, he wondered—if ever—should he return? With a companion, or without?—in urgent flight, in furtive secrecy or in confidence of a successful enterprise?

He looked over the bog at the dark line of the forest, and the sinister impression that he had known when first he saw it returned as a cloud crosses the sunshine.

There were dark things—dark and strange—that the island held, and the peril into which he went was beyond his estimate.

But he shook the foreboding from him, and went resolutely forward to the enterprise on which his desire was centred. For so men will, till the last sword is broken and the last maid is brought to motherhood. He went to dangers that he could not tell, and to a need that he could not know, for a vision of slim white limbs in the forest gloom and a head well carried—and for a voice in the night.

Charlton crossed the bog somewhat further to southward than he had done previously, and reached the shelter of the forest without difficulty. Continuing to the south, he came to the palisade of which Marcelle had told him. It must have been originally built of metal or of some very durable wood, but it was now a living wall of giant creepers and of clinging growths, with great trees branching over it. To a man who could climb, it presented no obstacle. Charlton went over without curiosity as to its structure. It was enough that it stood firmly, and had abundant footholds.

On the other side he found a difference. Beauty was there, as it had been in the forest; beauty of tree and bird, of flower and insect. It was as luxuriant as before, but it was curbed and tamed.

Trees fought for light and space in the forest. A score were choked, and one conquered. They took the shapes that the strife allowed. They had the vigour and the scars of their warfare. But here, each tree had its unrestricted space, its full shape. Every flower had its full value.

He had crossed the palisade about a mile further east than the pathway by which Marcelle had travelled. For the earlier part of the way he was distant from any dwellings, or the probability of observation. Now that the feast-night was approaching, the inhabitants were little likely to be wandering in such direction.

He did not know this, but he observed the quietude of the scene, and while he went forward watchfully, his rifle under his arm, he did not delay greatly for the finding of cover, thinking, indeed, that, should be come upon some wandering member of the community, it might be best that he should be seen advancing without evidence either of fear or hostility.

He had not gone far when he came upon some of the great birds of which Marcelle had told him. Remembering the assurance she had given that they were not dangerous, he walked quietly towards the nearest of these, and paused to observe its occupation. At a casual glance it might have been though that it was merely feeding upon the vegetation around it. But Charlton observed that its attention was confined to the overgrowth of a climbing plant with large white, bell-shaped flowers, like a giant bindweed, and that it was reducing it to an ordered shapeliness by the breaking-off of the pieces which it swallowed.

Further on, he came to a place where three of these birds were assembled around a young tree that showed a sickly appearance among the vigorous growths that surrounded it. He saw that they had cleared the soil from one side of its roots to a depth of a foot or two, and, while he watched, he observed one of them draw out an insect or reptile, like a huge millipede in appearance, about eighteen inches in length, and of the colour of sea-sand. Dropping it from his beak, he held it down with a toe across its neck while the three heads bent down to consider it. The birds appeared to consult in low squawking tones, and then, having apparently decided its fate whether the question was as to its deserts, its suitability for food, or which of them should have it, the captor lifted his claw, and before its myriad legs had hurried it more than a few inches away, the beak of one of the other birds caught it with an easy certainty and it was devoured in a moment.

Charlton had drawn near to the scene of this drama as it approached its conclusion, and now met the stare of the three birds as the three necks were turned in his direction.

He felt that they regarded him much as they had done the millipede that was now uncomfortably located in the nearest gizzard. There was a look in their eyes, at once amused and assured, which was disconcerting. Yet it was judicial rather than hostile, and he remembered that he had been told that they would not harm him. Probably they only regarded him with curiosity, as a member of the community whom they had not seen previously.

Charlton, like many men who are naturally unaggressive, was not easily frightened. He did not allow himself to deflect from the straight line of his direction, though it took him so near that a stretched neck could have reached him But, as he came close, they returned their attention to the work on which they had been occupied, and were filling up the hole around the root of the injured tree.

Charlton had neither the mental detachment nor the zeal for accumulating physical facts which would have dominated M. Latour under similar circumstances. Had he been informed that they belonged to the oldest of the extant orders of birds because they had no keel to the sternum, he would have been entirely unmoved, yet he looked on them with a lively interest as they resumed their labours.

In shape they were more like the cassowary than the ostrich, though they were somewhat taller, and much larger than the latter bird. Their bodies were longer than is that of the ostrich, and the wings lay more closely. The feathers were almost hair-like in texture. They lay closely, giving an appearance of a smooth compactness to the bodies they covered. Their colour was a neutral grey, with some silver pencilling, edged with black, on the wing-coverts. Their height was about six feet at the arch of the back, which was highest at the centre. They had not sufficient tail-feathers to break the downward curve of the back. Their necks were long, their heads, though really large, appearing small in consequence. One of the three—the one that had held the millipede under its claw while its fate was decided—had a kind of helmet of hard substance on its head, of a glossy green colour. The beaks of the other two, which he rightly supposed to be hens, were broader and flatter, and well adapted for the spadework in which they were occupied. Their dove-grey heads were smooth and feathered.

Charlton looked at these birds with a natural but transient interest. He had a settled purpose before him, and he had a feeling that he was engaged in something that was beyond his own volition.

Alert and wary, both of eyes and mind, he went on rapidly and without attempt at concealment. Approaching from a more easterly direction, he struck the main road into which Marcelle had adventured so abortively, just where the bushes commenced.

Clear in the half-dried mud at the roadside, he saw a naked footmark, such as he had first seen in the edge of the forest pool. These bushes were rarely more than four feet high, and they sloped downward to the bog. They grew closely, and he could look over them for half a mile, or perhaps more. He did not think anyone would make way far through them. It did not occur to him that anyone would attempt to crawl under them for any considerable distance. Seen by daylight, the idea was not reasonable.

He went along the road, watching the damper margin of the slimy soil beside it. By good fortune, he found the place where she had come out. The slants of the foot-marks at the two places were evidence that her direction had been similar to his own. He supposed that she had hidden, and had continued along the way when some danger had passed her. It was not quite correct, but Dr. Watson's simpleminded friend could have discovered no more, and would have wasted much time in the endeavour to do so.

Charlton paused at the second foot-mark. Marcelle's dimple would have shown more deeply than before, could she have watched him as he regarded it. But a foot-mark in the mud is not a token that the most infatuated lover can easily remove, or is likely to cherish, and this is more especially the case if he be in chase of the one who made it.

Charlton went on with a higher hope, a greater resolution, and an increased wariness. Whether in peace or peril, he had no further doubt that he was about to find her.

The path turned and fell. Its sides were wooded now. It turned again. He heard steps and voices approaching. He found time to consider that he ought reasonably to be frightened, and to observe that he was not, with a passing wonder. But knowledge is power. He wished to observe at leisure. He drew back behind a sheltering thicket.

CHAPTER TWENTY-ONE

THE WAITING

The old woman went to Jacob Sparrow. She said: "What is the meaning of *jamais*?" Jacob did not know. She said: "The girl looked at Demers through the lattice. She did not look pleased. She said: *'Jamais!—Jamais de la vie!'* " and turned away. She had been crying before. Afterwards, she did not cry."

Jacob did not know what to make of this, but he increased his precautions against her escape. Had she tried, she would have regretted it very quickly; but she did not do so.

The woman was far older than Jacob. He had been in her charge when his father left him on the island. He had some vague memories of his earlier years, but she alone had any clear knowledge of the civilisation that was beyond them. For many years she had been the nurse and doctor of the community. Now two younger women, who had previously assisted her, carried on the practice. It was the peculiarity of the island life that it was without organised religion. Priestcraft is responsible for many evils, as well as for much good. The conditions that prevailed here in its absence were its best vindication. But without some form of medical attendance they had found it impossible to exist.

There were superstitions, of course, vague and trivial, and individual rituals of grotesque kinds, but there was no organised religion, and consequently there was no flourishing heresy to contend against it.

The old woman was devoted to Jacob. Inclination and interest were in one scale. Demers hated her. If she watched Marcelle, it was not that she wished to assist his pleasure. But she was one of those to whom youth and all things youthful became hateful as the years advance. The reactions of age to the youth that succeeds it are the supreme evidences of character. Having a wider knowledge of life than those around her, she was the better able to judge what Marcelle's feelings were likely to be. But, like Jacob, she could not see that the girl had any alternative. It would be a sport to see her bent to his lust and brutalities. If she attempted to assert herself against him, the sport would be so much the greater. The old woman knew Demers. There would be something worth watching after the feast tonight.

Jacob sat at his door, as his custom was in the morning hours. He thought slowly as he drowsed in the sunlight, but his plans were clear and simple. He would make a speech tonight, which was a greater formality than was usually accorded to an island wedding. He would give this girl to his son, and he would decree that her children should succeed Demers, as Demers would succeed him. Perhaps, with that incentive she would be a real wife, and supply the brains of which he well knew his son's deficiency. The plan was not so base as its methods. And he would give Pierre his reward. When she had seen Pierre have his reward, she would not be in a mood for resistance. When they had drunk enough, if she were complacent, Demers could take her home. If not, the marriage could be consummated in the hall, as marriages, both willing and unwilling, had been before. It was a show worth watching. Of the scenes that went on at these monthly orgies, before they terminated in the drunken sleep of the feasters, it is best to say nothing.

Jacob felt that his plans were sound, and his conscience was untroubled. He drowsed in the sunshine.

Marcelle waited. She had decided not to attempt escape, unless a clear opportunity should offer. She waited and watched events, alert to seize any favouring change. She would meet the need of the moment as it arose. In the end, and till the last, she did nothing. The difference might have been little had she spent the day in despair or resignation, except in herself, which must be everything when the final judgement is taken.

She could not know that Jacob had decided that it would be best that Demers should not see her during the day, and she was in constant expectation that she might have to face him. Fainter, and more vague, was the hope that Charlton might be doing something to aid her.

To her the day passed slowly, though the evening would come too soon.

To Demers it was very long, for, in his own way, he was impatient to have her. Having slept off the effect of his exertions of the day before, he was hungry for the evening feast, and for the sport that would follow. He liked women in two ways. One was in thrashing them. He hoped for both enjoyments tonight. And the girl was finer than anything that the island offered. He rubbed an itching horn against the door-post on which he leaned. The day went slowly for Demers.

It is regarded as self-evident that time moves at the same pace for all of us, or, shall we say, that we can only move through it at the same pace and in the same direction. How else could an appointment be kept, or a date calculated? It is self-evident; and it is evidently false. There is a fallacy somewhere which is beyond the range of our intellects, like the question of the limitation of space, of which we can imagine neither boundary nor infinitude. If one man sits down to a game of cards, and another be tortured by a slow fire till the game be ended, will the time be the same for both?

It passed differently with the priest of Gîr, who lay in the purple gloom of the temple, before the altar that was old when the Nile Valley was unknown to men.

It was impossible to see clearly in the temple. The intensity of the colour which soaked the stones was like a mist in the unwindowed interior—a mist of colour which was neither red nor purple, and through which one looked with difficulty. The image of Gîr, towering to the roof, might be a statue or a mural painting. It was hard to tell. But its terror overcame the heart of the gazer.

The priest of Gîr did not look. He lay with his eyes darkened. His mind searched the ages that were past, and beat against the blind wall of the future. It was all over. His wife was dying. His race was dead. It would all pass at last. And yet not all. There was the child. Life would continue. Alien life, and yet the same. But all that had been, all its thought and all its wisdom would vanish. Though the books that the temple held should continue, there would be none that could read them.

And the world would still hold such flesh-eating filth as these creatures that were less than monkeys, and had destroyed his race with their diseases. Yet he need not die. He could avoid the issue that the mirror had shown him. Very easily he could avoid it. But the girl was not as these people. Neither had her father been such. Nor—though more doubtfully—was the man in the forest. And above all—there was the child. He rose, resolute. He would take the appointed path, and the rest was in the hands of Gîr. Was not Gîr the Maker of the world, and would he not control it to his own ends? Had not the All-god created him so that all it held and did, either of good or evil, was but the functioning of his spirit? Must not every world be as is the different spirit which the All-god gave to create it? Very dark and very bright was Gîr, and he had made the earth to his liking. Made it of blood and fire, of shadows and beauty. And its symbol was the sword. Peace comes, but the sword returns.

The priest of Gîr left the temple. He took a bronze-like sword, straight and sharp—a sword that had pierced the throats of many who had been doomed to death that the race might not degenerate. He fastened it beneath the looseness of the robe he wore.

He went in to his dying wife.

* * * * * * *

Ambushed in the thicket, beneath a canopy of dark-green leaves and heavy-scented heads of hydrangea-like blossoms, Charlton watched a straggling company of about a hundred men and women approach at a slow pace, with Jacob Sparrow at their head. Their numbers were about equal, for the excessive number of women who had been left on the island by Captain Sparrow had naturally not continued itself into the next generation. They moved slowly, for they could not exceed the pace which Jacob set at their head. Eight men came in a bunch behind them, two of whom carried muskets. As a precaution, though he thought it needless, Jacob had appointed these men to guard the door of the hall, two at a time, during the evening. Charlton looked at their weapons with some contempt. The ancient muzzleloaders were certainly slow and clumsy beside the rifle he carried—though they caused death and wounds enough at Waterloo or Marengo. He could not know that they were unloaded. Jacob did not purpose that the girl should be shot. Their purpose was to intimidate, and if that were insufficient, they were to be used to club anyone who should attempt to go either in or out without Jacob's permission during the evening. He had Pierre in his mind, as well as Marcelle. He remembered also the irruption of Jean on the previous occasion. In fact, he forgot nothing. He provided for everything, except for that of which he had no knowledge.

As a military demonstration, the eight men with the two muskets did not impress Charlton's mind very seriously, but he was conscious of a strange impression, which increased as he watched the procession that followed. It was such as may be felt by a caged, clean-feeding bird, which is given nothing but mouse-tainted corn for its hunger. In some indefinite way, the whole concourse was foul and unwholesome. To live among them would be intolerable. It would be nauseating to touch them. The women were squat and ungainly in shape, and course and brutish in aspect. Some were gaudily, and some grotesquely, dressed. A few were decorated with flowers. The men commonly wore cutlasses. A few had hatchets in their belts. These were sanguine individuals who hoped that a marrowbone might fall to their portion, and who were prepared to crack it.

Watching this procession, Charlton decided that they were only formidable by their numbers and their brutality. It might not be easy to establish friendly relations with such as they, even should he desire to do so.

Then he saw her. Among a knot of shorter women, toward the rear of the crowd. A small dark head. A skin sun-bronzed enough, but lighter than those around her. A face that was made for mirth rather than tragedy, but that showed a mood to equal the circumstance it had to face. He knew that it was she. He knew it by the quickened beating of his heart as he watched her. He would know it more surely still in a moment.

She came nearer, and he was aware of sea-blue eyes that were alert and searching. It seemed to him that their glances met. That must be fancy only, for he was so far drawn into the cover. Then she had passed. He did not venture to move, to observe her further. But he knew that he would follow her to hell, if the need were. And then her voice came, singing. They did not try to stop her. Why should they? There was no order that she should not sing the whole way, if she would.

"N'oserez vouz?
N'oserez vous?
N'oserez vous, mon bel ami?"

Had he doubted for a moment (which he would not own) the voice would have told him. And the song? Yes, he would dare. Very certainly, he would dare. But did it mean that she had seen him? He could not tell, but he thought she had.

CHAPTER TWENTY-TWO

THE REWARD OF PIERRE

The next hour went slowly for several of those whose fortunes we follow. Charlton had gained sufficient knowledge of the customs of these people to judge that they were on their way to the monthly feast, for which he had seen the meat provided on the previous day. He could not doubt, even without the evidence of the song, that Marcelle went unwillingly. He could not know the extremity or the urgency of her peril, but he was resolved to interrupt the proceedings, and to invite her to freedom. His reason told him that it would be best to let them settle down first before he intruded upon them, while his impatience denied it. His memory was not only of sea-blue eyes, or the defiant lift of a night-dark head. He had the vision also of one who had moved restlessly behind her. It was he whom he had seen club the panting satyr on the previous day, and then pull down the other for a facetious exchange of victims. Irked by the slow pace of the procession, he had been moving with long strides backwards and forwards behind her, his forward stoop and slouching motion showing him like a wolf that waits the moment to spring.

The time passed slowly for Charlton.

It passed slowly also for the priest of Gîr, who sat in the feast-house, waiting for the drama to open, the event of which he already knew.

How did it pass for the satyr, trussed now and roasted whole, and steaming at the top of the board? If we knew that, how much also should we know which is now hidden!

There was an appointed place for each in the feast-house. Jacob sat at the head, with Demers at his right hand.

At the head of each of the side-benches there sat a man to help with the carving. Below the man on the left the priest of Gîr would sit, with his wife opposite to him, in the places of honour.

The priest of Gîr and his wife always entered by a small side-door at the top of the hall, on Jacob's left hand, which was reserved for their use.

This evening he came alone. He explained with brief courtesy to Jacob that his wife was unwell. He did not say she was dead.

Jacob saw in this a convenience only. He gave her place to Marcelle.

The board was heaped with many fruits, and there were great vessels of the island wine.

Jacob and his son, with their two helpers, carved at different parts of the carcass, and the work of serving proceeded rapidly. The platters were green leaves, large and smooth and slightly concave. These leaves were destroyed when the feast was over. In this they had only adopted a custom which is prevalent in the islands of the Pacific. The unclean European custom of swilled earthenware had died out, if it had ever been practised among them.

Marcelle's position brought her close to the trussed body which was being carved so swiftly by long-practised hands. It was revolt-ingly human in its appearance. Indeed, the prevalence of cannibal-ism in the South Sea Islands suggests that these creatures may at one time have been generally distributed among them. When they died out, it would be natural for the frustrated appetites of their hunters to turn for satisfaction to their human enemies. Might it not even have been deduced that such creatures must have existed from the fact that cannibalism is so much more prevalent there than on other parts of the earth's surface?

Marcelle did not trouble herself with such speculations, but she had a shuddering memory of the fate which Jacob had threatened. It was unpleasant to think that she might be occupying the same posi-tion as the steaming satyr when the next month's feast should arrive. She put the thought from her mind.

Having such fears, and on the threshold of such a crisis, did she refuse to share in the feast? Could she attack the generous portion which Jacob carved for her benefit? The truth constrains me. She could. She was hungry, and she had a very practical mind. Here her Gallic ancestry told. For there is a difference.

A French woman may have a favourite hen, but if it should cease to provide her with expected eggs, she will give the accustomed call, and when it comes in confidence of a waiting meal, she will wring its neck without mercy, though not without regret. To her mind it is obvious. It is the only thing to be done.

An English woman is different. She will watch the hen, and know that it is no longer laying as it should, and say to herself that she ought to kill it, and put it off, and then one day a neighbour will tell her that she has a favourite hen that she ought to kill, but cannot bear to do it. And she will reply that she is in the same position. And then a bright idea will occur to one of them, and they will change the hens and both enjoy the dinners which will promptly follow.

A Frenchman could not be confronted by such a dilemma. He is not capable of a foolish affection for domestic poultry. An Englishman might have to face such a question, but he would solve it differently. He would let the hen live.

One must not imply any injustice to an exceptionally delightful girl. Marcelle was naturally affectionate, loyal, kind, and quick in sympathy, but she was not sentimental. She was inconsistent in many things, as we all are, and as those of mixed ancestry are particularly likely to be. (But this has been said before.) Certainly, she had no sentiment regarding a dead satyr. That it had a very human appearance when roasted would have seemed to her an absurd reason for refusing to take the place which was offered—as in fact it is. And having taken it, she found it so good that I am not prepared to say that she might not have asked for more—but other things supervened.

Eating went on steadily at first, and then slackened. Those who had carved were behind the rest, and must concentrate the more upon the portions which they had reserved for their own consumption. Words were few till the first half-hour had passed.

The priest of Gîr, eating lightly of the fruit before him, watched Marcelle's appetite with some speculation. It was important that he should understand her, and it was natural that he should be in some doubt as to her feelings and character. The mirror had shown him much, but it had not shown him the eyes that met her own from the thicket, nor could he understand why she looked so confidently at the fate which seemed about to seize her.

Marcelle looked at him with eyes which were equally speculative. He appeared cold and remote and, to her youthful eyes, very old. She did not think him likely to aid her. Yet she recognised that he was different from the others, a man to trust, as being free from any private baseness. But not one whose sympathy would deflect his judgement.

At Demers, though he watched her as his hunger slackened, she did not look at all. She was showing courage enough, but that was something that she could not do.

Avoiding him, she was inclined to look down the hall. It was the end of the first half-hour, and the guard at the door was changing, so that all might have their meals in turn. As they did so, six of the great rukas came in through the doorway, and sat down below the end of the table. There was nothing unusual in that. They came to be fed. It was in his boyhood that Jacob had discovered that they liked to pick the bones of the satyrs, and had commenced a practice which had now been established for half a century.

How they arranged it, who can say? But there were always six birds, neither more nor less, and they were all green-helmeted cocks; the hens did not come. The turn of these birds came when all had eaten and the carving was over.

Many years before, Jacob had rigged an ingenious device by which their meat could be hung in a large net-bag, at the sides of which they would peck, as the hens in a poultry run will peck at a hanging cabbage. It may have suited Jacob's youthful humour to see these sedate birds pecking between the strands of rope of which the bag was formed, while it swung away from them and was returned with an increased velocity by the pecks of their companions. The sides of the bag were of rope, but it had a bottom of leather, so that its contents should not fall out too freely. The leather foundation would lie flat and open on the floor, between the door and the foot of the table until the two carvers should carry down the great dish and tip the bony remnants upon it.

Then, by an ingenious contrivance of a seaman (long since dead) who had once been boatswain of the *Fighting Sue*, Jacob was able to pull a cord which hung over his chair, and the bag would be jerked up and drawn together at the top.

The rukas had learnt not to entangle themselves among the loose ropes, or to advance upon their meal until this had been done.

On this occasion, when the carvers had finished their own meal—which they were naturally the last to do—they would have risen to carry down the dish, but Jacob spoke a word to delay them. He then took a long drink of the island wine, and rose slowly to his feet to address the assembly.

He stood silent for a full minute, as his custom was, either to choose his words or because he had found that they gained weight when his hearers were kept in suspense. It was a tribute to his method that he never lacked the attention of his audience, and there was now a silence of expectancy. All were still, ceasing even to eat or drink, or reach for the fruit and wine which were before them.

Marcelle, thinking that the crisis had come, and resolute to resist, though with no clear plan of what she should speak or do, thought that they must hear the beating of her heart through the sudden silence of the hall.

She gave one glance down the double line of repulsive half-animal faces, but saw no hope of any help or understanding among them. Gluttony, indolence, disease, and dissipation were written there for a child to read them. Cowardice also on most, though some of the men showed an animal ferocity. Certainly there was none to whom she could appeal for any chivalrous help, none whom she would prefer even to Demers, none who would dare to challenge his anger, even were she prepared to reward him for such an adventure. All the faces, except that of Pierre's wife, who sat beside him at the very foot of the board, were marred by a lust of cruelty which was not animal, for animals are not cruel, with the very rarest exceptions, unless *Homo sapiens* be classified among them. It was subhuman, devilish. Different only was the priest of Gîr, whose eyes met her own for an instant, but she could read nothing from them. She felt that he understood: that he was watching, as a man watches a play. She knew that he was different from the rest. She felt instinctively that he had no sympathy with them. Had he sympathy with her? If so, would it move him to take part in the play? She was sure that he was fearless of them. She felt that he could help her. But she had no cause to think he would. Even Jacob, with all his cunning, in all those years, had never learnt what he thought.

Then she was aware that Jacob was speaking.

"Two years ago," he began, "we met to marry my son to a young woman who had been brought here for the purpose. We were interrupted. Then there was fighting, which need not have been, and men were killed, and she was frightened and ran into the forest. Now she has come back. She is a fine young woman, as you can see, though she might be thicker. She has improved since she ran away. My son likes her. My son has taken three other wives. That doesn't matter, if he wants another. You know I don't like any of you to have more than one wife. It makes quarrels, and there are not enough for all to have two. You can always change for a time, if you get tired of the one you have. But my son is different. He can have what he will. You can see he likes her." He glanced affectionately at the figure beside him, which was leaning forward gazing at Marcelle like a wolf withheld from his prey, his great teeth showing and his tongue licking the lips that never quite closed over them. "He can turn out the other three, or keep them, as he likes, though I expect he'll keep them. But this one will be his chief wife. I think she'll need some beating. Well, he can beat any woman without needing another to hold her down." He gave another glance of affection at his ungainly offspring. "When I'm dead, he will take my place, and if this young woman stays here, her son will take it after him." He paused again, and glanced at Marcelle who sat, white-faced and motionless, with no sign of hearing. "If she does what she's told, she'll be the first woman on this island. What she wants, she'll have, and no one will lay a hand on her except her husband. If she tries to go back to the woods, I've told her that we shall all share her." He tapped the dish before him, and his tone, though jocular, had a note of merciless warning. "We'll have her skinned and lying here on the next feast-day. But she hasn't come back for that." He paused again, and Marcelle wondered whether she were to be handed over immediately, and the crisis was upon her. But he went on, with a different note in his voice, and her breath came again. "But the first thing is to pay a debt that has been owing for two years. I always do what I promise. There was a man who came and said that he could find a wife for my son who would be better than any of the women here, if I would give him one of these bars of gold when he had brought her. Well, here she is—and he shall have his reward." He paused again, and then bent down to his son and said something in too low a voice to be overheard even by those nearest. Then he continued: "We don't allow slaves up here, and it's too far to throw, so as my son gets the woman, he shall take him the reward."

He sat down with a smile on his face, and Demers rose and took one of the gold bars from the pile that lay just below the great dish. He went down the right side of the hall, where Marcelle and her father had once hurried with the cutlasses thrusting as they passed.

The hall was silent, and heads were turned in a dull puzzlement. Why had the gift not been passed down, and why had Jacob chosen his son as the messenger? And why did Demers, who had no love for his father, obey the order with such alacrity?

But though Demers went at once, and with a seeming willingness, he did not hand the gift with any goodwill when he reached the foot of the hall. Pierre had risen, and stood with bent head to receive it. He looked as meek as ever. His mind was divided between satisfaction at getting the coveted gold, and a vague unrest arising from the tone in which it was given.

Demers stopped a few paces from him. He raised the golden bar as though he were about to fling it in the face of the carpenter. He addressed him with abusive island words for which there are no exact English substitutes, and there is no need to paraphrase them: he accused him of having known where the girl was all the time, and kept her from him. He described what he would do to Pierre, but for his father's orders. Then he threw the brick.

Pierre raised a shielding arm, but it did not hit him. It fell in the leather centre of the bag, and Demers laughed and went back up the hall.

Pierre hesitated a second, uncertain whether there were some malicious intention underlying the position to which the bar had been thrown. He knew well that there was no goodwill in the gift, either from father or son. But if he left it there till the bag were drawn up, it might not be too large for one of those monstrous gullets to swallow. Perhaps Demers had hoped that one of the birds would attempt to do so, seeing it in that position. But they did not move. They never advanced till the bag was drawn up. They were sitting quietly now, larger than camels, placid as resting geese. Pierre stepped forward to take his prize, and as he stooped to raise it, Jacob pulled the rope.

CHAPTER TWENTY-THREE

"SHE IS MY WIFE"

The bag was large, but Pierre was a large man, and it was not intended for such a burden. He was jerked off his feet by the first pull, yet he made a struggle to free himself; and though the cords contracted almost instantaneously as it was raised from the ground, he got one arm out of the top, where it did him no good, the cords closing so tightly that he was unable to use or withdraw it. For the rest, it closed around him till he was drawn into a ball, the caught arm rendering it impossible for any struggles to alter his position appreciably, even had the tightness of the net been insufficient to hold him. The spasmodic efforts which he made caused him to swing and spin in a manner which roused the excited amusement of the spectators, as did the cries with which he begged for release and mercy.

So far it was comedy only, however heartless, but the victim's cries rose to a shrill scream as he became aware that the rukas had risen, as they were accustomed to do when the net was drawn up, and were advancing upon him.

They surrounded the swaying bag, evidently curious and uncertain of the unusual meal which it offered. It hung at about the level of their heads, and as it had a leather bottom it was only through the sides that they could reach its contents.

Pierre was fastened so tightly now that in some places he bulged slightly between the cords. One of the birds made a doubtful peck, and the bag swung round towards another. This one pecked more boldly. Its beak showed a piece of tom cloth, as the bag swung away like a pendulum. Another bird jumped at it with half-open wings, and there was a great wisp of Pierre's beard in his beak as the bag swung away in another direction.

To this point Marcelle had watched with no great horror. She had no cause to love the carpenter, and he had been receiving the price for which he had betrayed her when the jest was played upon him. That it was anything more than a cruel jest she had not imagined. But at the scream he gave as the hair was torn out, she forgot everything, even her own peril, in indignation and protest.

"Oh, stop it! Stop it!" she exclaimed, turning from the sight of the horror with a glance that included both Jacob and the priest of Gîr. But the latter was looking on with an expression which showed no sympathy. He did not appear interested in the carpenter's fate, but looked on as an actor waiting in the wings to take his part in the tragedy.

Jacob was leaning forward, gripping the edge of the table with thick red fingers, his face showing an excitement such as he rarely exhibited, while his age-dimmed eyes strove to miss nothing of the drama which was being played as he had planned that it should be.

He did not notice her protest.

The whole assembly was in a state of uncontrolled emotion. They were half risen from the seats, leaning forward to get a clearer view, gesticulating, and talking to neighbours who did not heed them.

Then came a scream of shriller agony from the swinging net, as one of the great birds pulled away a mouthful which was neither clothes nor hair. Demers had returned to the top of the hall, walking backward that he might lose nothing of the sight as he did so. He was behind Marcelle as Jacob first showed that he was aware that she was addressing him, now with a roused passion of pleading against the torture which they were witnessing. He spoke more quickly than usual, and with a slurred intonation, as though drunk with the excitement of the spectacle. "He is getting what he deserved. It will be a lesson to you." He looked at Demers. "Take her away. She's yours now. She won't be much trouble now she's seen how we deal with misbehaviour."

Demers dropped a huge black-haired hand on her shoulder. "Come along," he said roughly, looking down upon her with an animal hunger that had no trace of love, nor any chance of mercy.

Suddenly the expected crisis was on her. She resisted an impulse to sink her teeth in the hairy fingers that gripped her. She rose from the bench and faced him. The horror that she had witnessed, the excitement around her, had given her a strange exaltation of spirit, in which she heard her own voice in words which she had not consciously intended. "Why do you want me?" she asked, and looked with a fearless quietude into the face that bent toward her. Always she would remember the black hair, coarse and long, on the left side of his head where the short horn showed through it. Demers was not good at argument, or rather his arguments were of a direct and forcible order. "Come along," he repeated, but in a voice that was now a growl of menace. He gripped her shoulder again, and at the touch her control left her, and in a sudden passion of repulsion she struck the hand away. She had not lived in the forest boughs for two years without the hardened muscles of her arms, soft and round though they might appear, having gained a strength that many men might have envied. Anger and fear released this strength to its limit. Demers' hand fell, his wrist numbed where the blow had struck it.

But it could only be the success of a moment. Demers stood over her, grinning in anticipation of the payment which he would give for her attempt at resistance. She was surrounded by evil faces that would take delight in her degradation. They were turned already from the horror at the foot of the hall where the birds were now burying their beaks in a meal which had almost ceased to scream, and from which the blood was spouting over them as they tore it. But the spectators were anticipating another exhibition which would be equally pleasurable to witness. Jacob looked at his son. "You had better break her here," he said, while Marcelle looked round like a trapped hare for any means of escape that might offer.

She looked at the priest of Gîr, but he was not looking at her. Her eyes followed his, and stopped fascinated. Demers, his hands raised to seize her, stopped also, as an unfamiliar voice said with a quiet assurance: "You cannot do that. She is my wife."

Charlton, who had entered by the little door which the priest used, stood a few feet behind Jacob's chair. Till he spoke, no one had seen him, their attention having been turned to Marcelle when it was drawn from the execution at the other end of the hall.

Jacob, turning round in his chair, saw a young man with a rifle, ready, though not threatening, in the crook of his arm, and an air of cool assurance, that warned him to the exercise of his natural caution.

For the moment audacity triumphed. Jacob thought quickly. He must have come from the outer world, and if one had come, there might be fifty. He had not forgotten the deadly use which Marcelle's father, whom they had thought unarmed, had made of the little weapon he carried.

He looked at Demers, who had been paralysed by surprise into a pause of inactivity. "Wait," he said, "I will deal with this," and then to Marcelle: "Is it true?"

If the girl hesitated, it was for so short a time that it was not perceptible to those who watched her. "Yes," she said. What else could she?

Jacob did not believe her. Why had she not told him before, if it were so? He was aware of the rifle at his back, and he wished to avoid an instant crisis. When he had learnt more, he would know what to do.

He looked at Charlton again. He said: "We must talk of these things. Will you sit with us?" He told one of the carvers to give place, leaving a vacant seat between him and the priest of Gîr. He did not wish Charlton to be on the same side as Marcelle.

Charlton advanced at once, and took the offered place. He sat down with the rifle between his knees. The sword-hilt showed over his shoulder. He looked armed and unafraid. He was alone among a hundred enemies. But they did not know that he was alone. Not yet. When they did....

He looked round at the rows of evil faces turned in his direction. They were silent now, watching him with a hostile but puzzled curiosity.

Marcelle, at a word from Jacob and a nod from Charlton, had resumed her seat. Demers had returned to his place at his father's side. He said nothing, but regarded Charlton with a murderous stare, which left no doubt of its meaning.

He did nothing as yet because, though he had no love for his father, he knew that he could depend upon him to provide his wishes more cunningly than he could do for himself. He scowled, and waited.

There was a short silence while the old man appeared to ruminate, looking down on his hands. He looked half-somnolent. Charlton began to wonder if they were accepting the position which he had claimed. The ease of his victory seemed incredible. Then the old man looked up again, and commenced speaking slowly and reasonably.

"It is two years since the young woman was brought here by her father to be a wife to my son, to which she agreed. Since then she has been lost in the woods. That is her own tale. Now she comes back and says she is still willing to marry him. She says nothing of having fled from another husband. Can you explain?"

Charlton saw his difficulty. He did not know what she might have told already. He saw that the truth might not help them. He saw the cunning that said little, but threw the danger of words upon his own shoulders. He answered with similar reticence, and with a question which touched the weakest point in the indictment: "Did she escape?"

Jacob felt the coolness of the parry, but he was not simple enough to be drawn from his position to give battle on his opponent's ground.

"As I see it," he said, "she is my son's wife. If you claim her, it is for you to explain."

Charlton could not explain. He knew that, and Jacob guessed it. He answered easily: "You have heard her admit that she is my wife. I do not know what may have happened two years ago, but I know of some things which have happened since. But does it matter? Neither of us would wish to claim her against her will. If she says that she prefers your son, he can have her. There is no need to quarrel. If she prefers to come back to me, I am content. I will not ask what may have kept her here."

Jacob was silent again. He wished to know whether this man were alone. He had been long on the island? Could he leave it at will? He wondered whether the priest of Gîr knew anything of him. He could not ask without being overheard by the man who sat between them. Nor could he give orders for him to be surrounded and overpowered without an instant danger, both to himself and Demers. He did not answer Charlton at once, but turned and whispered to Demers, who rose and went down to the end of the hall. He passed the feeding birds, and said something to the two men at the entrance, who laid their muskets down and went out with him.

Charlton guessed that this movement had some sinister intention, and wondered whether he would do well to force the issue before they should return, and then Jacob spoke again: "The young woman has chosen my son, and, as you say, that is final. There is really no need to ask her, but as you wish, I will do so. I have no doubt that she will reply as she should." He was not so confident as he professed to be, but he considered that everything might be gained, and nothing need be lost by this test. He knew that Demers was hurrying with one of the men to fetch powder and ball and loaded muskets, which would place the intruder at an augmented disadvantage, and that the other was searching the vicinity for any sign of a larger invasion. He would soon have firearms in the hall. He would soon know whether the stranger were alone. He turned to Marcelle: "Do you wish to go with this man, or will you keep your word to my son?"

The words were quiet and slow. Only the eyes menaced with a glance at the bone-strewn dish before them, of which Charlton could not understand the meaning. But Marcelle knew.

She looked back with an aspect of courage, trying to speak, and aware of an inward panic which left the words unformed. Her glance turned to Charlton. Gaining there what she sought, she said: "I would rather go." She knew, as the words were uttered, that the final choice was made, and that she was married to this three-days stranger, as neither church nor priest, nor any physical contact had power either of divorce of union. For the divinity of marriage, whether it be of a wood-dove or of a woman, is in freedom of choice, and in a subsequent loyalty, without which nothing can sanctify, and with which nothing can degrade it.

She said: "I would rather go," and rose as she said it.

It was her instinct to seek the protection of the man whom she had chosen.

Charlton rose also. There was a joy of victory in his heart, and his eyes were alert and confident.

Jacob showed no sign of resentment, but answered slowly: "She has twice chosen my son. Now she says that she has chosen you. It is a matter which cannot be decided in my son's absence. He will be back in a few minutes. You must wait till he returns. He has a right to know what is decided." For the first time he addressed the priest of Gîr: "It is not just that we should await his return?"

In the doubt as to whether Charlton were alone, or one of many potential enemies, it was natural that Jacob should wish to know whether he could count upon the support of the priest, and of the unseen people who were supposed to live in their southwestern reservation, and the question was very cunningly addressed to him on a point of procedure, on which Jacob felt that the priest's concurrence might be readily given; but there was no warrant of support in the coldly courteous answer which he received. "They might ask 'Why did he go?' But it may be best to wait."

Hearing it, Charlton felt an added assurance. Here was a personality as remote as his own from the foul crowd around him, and yet serene and unfearing. He saw also that there was an appearance of justice in Jacob's contention, and that it would certainly be more dignified, and might even be safer, to wait and listen to anything which Demers could urge on his own behalf, than to attempt to force a hurried exit before his return. He felt it essential that they should avoid an aspect of haste or fear.

He said. "We will wait, if you wish," and then to Marcelle: "There is room here," and made space for her on the bench beside him, the priest also moving with the same object.

Marcelle came round the head of the table very quickly, before Jacob had considered any course of prevention, which would have been difficult without resort to immediate violence, which he aimed to avoid.

Charlton felt that he had gained much, for his mind was on the side-door behind them, and Marcelle was now as near as he, and, being beside him, he could give her a hint which would be unheard by others. He began to consider the probable result of a sudden retreat in that direction, and to estimate the probable action, and survey the weapons, of the men that were nearest.

It was just then that one of the rukas gave a high call—a call so loud that it could be heard not only in the hall, but half a mile away. Jacob knew this call well. It was one by which the leading birds would summon their companions for the tasks of the garden. But it had never been heard in the hall before. Now they heard it repeated in the gardens outside. Three times they heard it. It meant nothing to Charlton. It puzzled Jacob. It only told the priest of Gîr that the mirror had not mistaken the course which events would take. It was forgotten by all as Demers came back through the doorway.

He came with a man behind him carrying an armful of loaded muskets and a bag of powder and ball. He made no attempt to conceal these. They were distributed at once to those who guarded the door and to others around.

He had learnt that the stranger was alone, at least in that neighbourhood, and he had returned resolved to settle matters by such ways as he understood, if his father should not have done so already by his different methods. He wore a belt now, with a heavy cutlass and two horse-pistols. He looked up the hall and saw Marcelle seated beside Charlton. She was peeling a red-skinned banana with an appearance of ease which she may not have felt.

Demers came up the hall with long strides, his body slouching forward and his head projecting, as was his way when he walked. His teeth were set, and his face was flushed with blood. Charlton saw that there was something different from Jacob here—something which could not be fenced off with words or adroit delayings. Demers stopped at the head of the table, and looked at Charlton. His glance was murderous, with the ferocity of a beast of prey. He looked at Marcelle, and his eyes changed to a greed of anticipation. She would suffer for this. No, he would not need his other wives to hold her down when he beat her. He had little imagination, and none that was not based on his appetites, but he felt that his hand was in her hair already.

The satisfaction of the thought may have been the restraint which withheld him from one of the uncontrollable furies to which he was liable. Charlton thought that he would leap at him over the table. He had his own right hand in his jacket pocket, and wondered whether a revolver-shot would be sufficient to stay him. He would have no time to adjust the rifle. He did not like the thought of those hands on his throat.

But Demers did not leap. He said. "Will you fight or go? Shall I kill you first, or will you watch while I beat her?" He did not notice the hand which Jacob raised, or hear the words which were meant to restrain. Jacob saw that the course which his cunning had planned was becoming impossible.

Charlton, cooler than his opponent, though with an almost equal willingness to kill, was reminding himself that to lose his own life was to leave the girl at the mercy of the beast before him. He was resolved that he would not rashly incur such a hazard. He only said, "How?"

Demers extended hairy hands in silent and sufficient answer. Charlton was silent. He would be a fool indeed to give himself to be tom or choked in that beast-like grip. The derision of the thought may have come into his eyes and been the spark which lighted the sudden rage of his enemy. There was a knife, long and sharp, which had been used for the carving, lying on the table beside him, and this he caught up and flung at Charlton from his three-yards distance with deadly force and accuracy. It came from a skilled hand in a craft the practice of which was inherited from the blood of his Chilean grandmother, and was much used in the island. As the knife spun through the air it was a thousand chances to one that Charlton's life was ended. There was no possible time to move aside, nor to think of any means of protection, but with a blind, swift instinct the hand that held the upright barrel of the rifle raised it in an effort of protection which might have appeared absurd in its futility had there been time for thought; and by a chance which was on the verge of the miraculous, the point of the flashing blade was caught and deflected on the narrow shield of steel. Charlton was aware that the rifle was almost knocked from his grasp, and then saw the knife quivering in the neck of the priest beside him.

The priest said nothing. He raised his hands and drew out the knife. The wound was neither deep nor dangerous. The force of the throw had been broken when it was turned aside. It had struck him where the muscle of the neck joins the shoulder. He showed no concern, though it bled freely. He looked at Charlton and at the girl beyond him. "Come with me," he said, and the three rose together. Charlton had drawn the revolver from his pocket and watched Demers, ready to shoot at the first movement that threatened danger, but reluctant to do so if it could be avoided. Jacob stared at them, seeming about to speak, but no words came. Even Demers appeared to be taken aback for a moment by the result of his murderous throw. Since long before his own birth the priest of Gîr had sat in that place, remote, austere, different from themselves, but by his presence giving an assurance of amity between them and the unseen inhabitants of the temple precincts.

It was a pause that might have burst into violence at the next instant, had there not come a scream of fear and agony—and then another—from the lower end of the hall. They were such cries as Pierre had given when the great birds tore his flesh from him, and every eye was turned to the place from which they came, but with different feelings from those which had found a hectic enjoyment in the dying agonies of the carpenter.

For while the general attention had been drawn to the altercation between Demers and Charlton at the upper end of the hall, there had occurred a scene without precedent at the lower doorway, where a dozen of the great birds had crowded in at the call of their companions, to pick the bones of the carpenter.

The men who stood with loaded muskets at the door had made no attempt to stop them, though they were alarmed and puzzled by the novelty of the invasion, for it was well understood that their movements should not be molested. But others were seen to be approaching, and the space between the door and the foot of the table was already crowded with these birds in a condition of unwonted excitement, including some hens, none of which had previously entered the hall, when there came the cries which drew all eyes in their direction.

Introduced, as they had been, to a diet of human flesh—invited to tear to pieces a man that was clothed and living—their appetites roused and unsatisfied—it was not surprising that some of them began to stretch investigating heads towards the men and women that were seated nearest.

These people had been taught from childhood, and had learned by experience, that, if they left the birds alone, they would not be attacked by them. They were not quick to fear, but they shrank and moved uneasily as the long necks stretched among them. And then at the end of either of the long side-benches, at the same moment, the assault came. At one a man gave a single scream that choked as a bird's beak closed on his throat and dragged him backward from the bench among the eager beaks of its companions. At the other, scream followed scream as a great beak which had been feeling round a man's feet, pushed upward beneath his tunic and buried itself in his body. The man fell from the bench, struggling vainly, the bird holding him down with one foot while it fed. His nearest comrades made no effort to rescue him, but drew back in panic, only baring the cutlasses which they appeared always to wear on these occasions, and slashing the air to discourage the further advances of the necks that were stretched toward them.

Then a man by the door fired his musket, and one of the birds fell. It kicked furiously on the ground, making a great outcry. Then it regained its feet, and stood swaying unsteadily. Charlton could not see where it was hit.

Some of the birds gathered round it curiously. Others— probably the later-comers whose appetites were unsatisfied— crowded to feed upon the two victims that had been pulled down.

Charlton noticed the satyr-footed wife of Pierre, who had been seated beside him. When he was given to the birds, she had fallen unconscious from the cross-bench at the foot of the table. There she still lay, faint or dead, but the birds did not touch her.

The priest of Gîr looked on as one who watches a familiar scene. He appeared aloof as ever, concerned neither for the bleeding wound in his own neck, nor for the torments of the wretches that were being eaten alive at the further end of the hall. Yet he had drawn a sword from beneath his garment, and held it in an awkward-seeming manner in his left hand. But it was the way to which he had been trained, and the appearance was deceptive.

Jacob sat motionless, gazing with his failing eyes at the tragedy that he had originated. Always more adroit to avoid than to meet a crisis, he made no attempt to control the situation.

Demers, cursing inarticulately, had run down the hall, a pistol cocked in his hand. Courage he never lacked, and such brains as nature had given him were always stimulated by a call to action. "Stand your ground, fools—slash at their necks," he bellowed, stopping their flight by the confidence of his voice and with the persuasion of a hard-driven fist where it was needed.

But the birds had not followed them up the hall. They appeared to consult together around the one that was wounded. They did not seem to be either frightened or angered, but, as though they realised a serious position which required further reflection, they made an orderly retreat from the hall. They called to those that were still feeding, and these withdrew reluctantly with blood-drenched heads from their ghastly banquets.

Then several things happened very quickly.

Charlton, who might have used the chance to retreat with Marcelle through the door behind him, had watched fascinated for one foolish minute, his instinct being to take sides with his own kind, however base or hostile, against such an attack. He had even thrown his rifle forward, and would have fired could he have got a safe shot above the heads of the moving crowd.

Marcelle's more practical female mind suffered from no such confusion. Had she stood alone, she would have been through the door, and in swift flight to her familiar trees at the first moment of opportunity. But she had chosen her lover, and she left the control of their movements in his hands without protest, though with impatient eyes.

As the birds turned away, she heard the voice of the priest of Gîr. He addressed her quietly, but with a deliberate slowness, so that the words would neither be confused nor forgotten. "You will take the path you know, and the steps in the south end of the temple. Lose no time. The birds will not harm you. I give the child to your keeping." She did not know what he meant, and there was no time to reply.

Charlton's hand was on her arm, and he was drawing her to the door. Even at that moment a memory woke in her of how she had thrilled to him, as she did now, when he touched her foot in the darkness.

Jacob saw the movement. He opened his lips to call to Demers to stop them. His eyes met those of the priest of Gîr, and the words were unspoken. The next moment they were unspeakable.

With a swift, strong backward sweep, the priest's sword had reached his neck. The keen thin blade, impelled by the full strength of the practised arm, passed completely through it, and was not checked in its course. There was a second during which Jacob sat with a stunned mind, not knowing that he was dead. He tried to rise, but the thought came too late for the severed nerve to convey it, or he might have walked headless, as a fowl will do in the like case. He gazed down at the hands that would not move as he willed them, and as the shock lessened he was aware of a fire of pain around his neck. He saw his body slip sideways beneath him. His head rolled on the table.

It was over in an instant. We may suppose that he lost consciousness very quickly, as the blood drained from the severed head. Knowing nothing, we may suppose what we will. But there is some reason to doubt it.

It was at the same instant that the priest of Gîr fell forward as a musket-shot sounded from the lower end of the hall. It was not fired with any purpose to harm him, but from a trigger pulled in panic by one of the sentries at the door as the birds crowded out, and he had mistakenly thought that one was about to seize him.

Charlton saw the priest fall, and turned back, though Demers was already running up the hall with a rabble of followers more willing to attack a single man than they had been to face the beaks of the rukas.

The priest looked up. There was no friendship in his eyes, nor surprise, nor any fear. He was remote as a god. He said: "I am killed. Go quickly. There is the child." Charlton thought that he meant Marcelle. He remembered her peril, and went.

He ran through the door, pushing Marcelle before him and swinging her aside as he passed it, out of the line of fire. He heard the explosion of Demers' horse-pistol as he did so. Standing aside, he put an arm round the door and fired his revolver three times in rapid reply. Blind though the shots were, he judged that they could scarcely fail of effect on the advancing crowd, and at the best would check them, as indeed they did, though not for more than a minute, for their flight was seen and shouted by others who had run from the main door.

"Run for the trees," he said. "I can keep them back here." But she shook her head. Her voice trembled into laughter. "I can run faster than you."

He saw that she would not go alone, and ran with her. They would have gone due north, by the side of the hall, and toward the distant safety of the forest, but the men who ran out of the front would have cut them off. Hearing that they were on the run, Demers came with his followers through the side-door. The spreading line of pursuit was forcing them toward the temple grounds.

They heard the sound of Demers' remaining pistol. It was a useless shot at the distance which they had gained. Musket-shots followed, but there was little precision in those ancient weapons, and, whether well or badly aimed, the bullets did not come near them.

Marcelle ran the more easily, for the two years of forest life had given muscles and breath that the advance of civilisation had left behind, and she was lightly clad and unburdened, but Charlton's longer stride kept beside her.

Gaining the shelter of some scattered trees, he turned in hope to check pursuit with his rifle. The chase was scattered now, there being only three that were near them, with Demers twenty yards farther back, and the rest straggling over a space of two hundred yards behind.

Charlton fired twice, and the foremost pursuers paused. He was not sure that he did any damage, though he thought that one man shook a bleeding hand.

Demers, stooping to a thicket's shelter, reloaded his pistols.

Charlton would have fired again, but Marcelle called to him that they were being surrounded while they stood, for though they had checked the progress of those who were directly behind them, there were others running far to right and left who did not slacken.

Then they ran again, faster for the breath they had gained, and down a turfy slope, where speed was easy. Here they gained on those who were on their left, as the ground there was less favourable, but on their right, between them and the forest, the pursuers had made better way, and their retreat was now cut off entirely. They must go straight on towards the temple, or turn to the unknown land that stretched to the southward cliffs, where there might, most probably, be the same boggy hollows which they had learnt to dread on the eastern side.

They were going uphill now, at a slackened speed. Here they showed plainly to their pursuers, and the muskets sounded.

Over the ridge they paused, looking round for the best way to take. Life and death might hang on the choice of the straight path or the trammelled way. "I know," she said, and ran on with a fresh courage. She had seen the way which she had gone with her father two years before, and knew that they were on the shortest track, where all must be as strange to their enemies as to themselves.

Charlton spurted, and came level. "Did you mean it?" he asked, surprisingly. Their glances met, and she did not pretend to mistake him. "But no!" she said, with eyes that laughed and mocked and challenged. He caught her hand in reply, and they ran on together with a new speed and lightness.

The path they were now on ran straight forward. Its surface was a lawn-like turf. At times it was closed in by a luxuriance of flowering bushes, or by groups of trees, of which each one, in an ordered peace, was given light and air for its full growth, relieved from the fierce pressure of the forest strife and the stranglehold of its creeping parasites. They had a great, though a different, beauty. They bore no scars, they were of an untested valour. Their growth was of a complete symmetry. They had fulfilled themselves, as they could not have done in the stress of the forest life. They demonstrated the blessings of peace. And yet—their peace was founded on the ruthless destruction of all that would have competed around them. Life was less here than in the forest—certainly less in its total, perhaps less in its degree. It is the insoluble problem. War is evil—and without evil there can be no good.

But the trees reached mighty trunks aloft, and found free air and light abundant, and the warmth of the tropic sun. Did they look far off and scorn the savage trees that fought for life in the forest? Or did they envy? Would the lightning strike them at last, that might have spared had they not risen so high and so apart?

A few months before, Charlton, sick of life and its futilities, had lounged on a hotel veranda—Marcelle had dreamed and longed in the safety of the forest boughs.

Now they ran for their lives—war had found them—love and war together. If they escaped at all it would be with the blood of others on their hands. Were they less or more than they had been? Were they blessed or cursed by the net of circumstance that had caught them? God knows, who made the world and all its wonders.

It is only sure that neither of them would have gone back had the choice been offered. They had found violence and peril which they did not seek, but they had found love also, and, by the paradox of God, love was a better thing than it could have been had Marcelle yielded to the hand that touched her in the forest night, or had Charlton been deaf to her pleading.

CHAPTER TWENTY-FOUR

THE FLIGHT

They ran on in good hope of safety, though they knew that they were half-surrounded. Perhaps the greatest doubt in Charlton's mind was the reception which they would meet should they attempt the forbidden sanctuary of the temple that now rose in plain sight before them, a pile of square-built ruby-coloured stone that glowed intense in the sunlight

It was surprising that pursuit had followed into this forbidden territory, but it had been led by the blind fury of Demers; and the death of Jacob and the priest, the revolt of the rukas, and the spectacle of their ghastly meals, had roused a frenzy of excitement to which these people were liable, a frenzy which affected them as a mob rather than as individuals, and had some of the effects of courage. There was also the idea in the mind of Demers that the strangers must be prevented at any cost from carrying the news of the priest's death to those who (he supposed) might be roused to avenge it. Sooner or later, in some way, he supposed that it must be told. But if the stranger were killed, might not the guilt be laid at his door? Might they not say that they had killed him to expiate the outrage he had committed? And then he wanted the girl. He wanted her the more because she loathed him. He intended to violate her, but his first desire was to feel her shrink from his hands, and to beat her into submission.

Though he had little intelligence, he was a cunning fighter enough. He had no code of honour to encumber his mind. He wished to kill, and to capture. He had no intention of being killed if he could avoid it. He could have run faster than he did, having more endurance than most of his followers. The pace of all—pursued and pursuers—had gradually slackened as the miles were passed, but when he found that he would have outdistanced his companions had he kept straight on, he made a slanting junction with those who were attempting to outflank the runners on the southern side.

Such was the position when they came in full sight of the temple.

At this point the path was hedged on either side by some flowering shrubs, ten or twelve feet in height. They had very dark green leaves, tinged with scarlet, and great balls of cream-hued blossom of the size of a man's head. These were not easy to penetrate, but could they do so, they would make direct for the southern end of the temple. Marcelle remembered the words of the priest. They pushed through them. They were abused by a colony of dark green paroquets, with lighter chests tufted with white, that made the bushes their home. These mentioned with emphasis that "Belgium was a country, not a road," but they lacked allies, or even a treaty. Their nests were ruined, and there were no reparations. Such is war—in another aspect.

Emerging on a higher path, they met a child. It may be, though it is not sure, that Charlton might have passed her. But Marcelle stopped. The child was about three years old. She was dark-eyed, slender, olive-skinned, with an exotic beauty of the kind that does not change with the years. She walked as one who is lost and bewildered, and yet goes on with a purpose. She stopped when they came out of the bushes. She looked at them with eyes that were wild and shy, but she did not retreat.

Marcelle spoke to her, telling her she must not go that way. What fate might not be hers from the savage crowd that pursued them? The child looked with uncomprehending eyes. She said something in a strange tongue. The tone was plaintive, the words evidently a question, but they meant nothing to those who heard.

Charlton looked troubled. "We mustn't wait," he said doubtfully.

"We can't leave her here," Marcelle answered.

They looked up the path, they even called through the bushes, but she seemed to be quite alone.

Marcelle reached out her arms, and the child hesitated and then came. Marcelle lifted her, and the child trembled a little and then clung closely. She made no sound, but Marcelle saw that there were tears on the long dark lashes. She thought of the baby monkey that she had left in the trees. "Come on," she said, and began to walk forward. Charlton was refilling the empty chambers of his rifle.

"You know it means they'll catch us," he said.

"We couldn't leave her," Marcelle answered. "Could we?"

He said: "Very well. But let me carry her."

"No," she answered. "She's not heavy. You must be free for anyone that needs killing."

There was a fierceness in her voice which he had not heard before. There was a blend of hardness and tenderness in her nature which would often baffle him in the days to be.

He had the sense not to argue. They went on at a quick walk.

He felt sure that there would be fighting now, and he began to calculate the men and weapons that he might have to meet, and to think how best he could counter them.

Could they find ambush where there would be an open space around them, wide enough to be out of the range of muskets? He was confident that his rifle could hold them back under such conditions, as long as his ammunition should last. But after?

There was one thing in their favour. The night was coming. It is significant of how much longer these events have taken to tell than to act that it had not fallen already. It was not yet four hours since he had heard the voice that asked *"N'oserez vous?"* to one who hid in the thicket.

If they could lie concealed now, the darkness might help them to a further flight, and to safety.

Could they reach the temple burdened as they were? It did not look to be very far, but such appearances are sometimes deceptive.

What reception would they meet if they gained its shelter?

The child might help. But what if there were no one there who could understand them? The priest had been able to speak the corrupt English of those he met, but it was clearly not his official language.

Or suppose that these people should attempt to seize Marcelle, after the manner of Demers?

It seemed to Charlton that they went from danger to danger.

His mind was on the forest, the cliff, the safety of the caves—and of the waiting boat.

But Marcelle's thought was different. The temple was her goal. She had an instinct that it would be the place of their security. She did not vex her mind with imagination of who might receive them, or in what way. She knew that the priest of Gîr had been a different quality from those from whom they were flying. She remembered the words which had seemed unmeaning when she heard them: *"You will take the path you know, and the steps in the south end of the temple. I give the child to your keeping. "*

Well, she had the child, and she would go to the temple. It was Charlton's part to help her to get there. She did not doubt he would do so. She trusted him as she had once trusted her father.

She did not know that Demers crouched in a thicket a hundred yards ahead, with a loaded pistol in either hand.

He fired the first one too soon. He was not a very skilful or practised shot—Jacob had not allowed the use of powder except for the actual hunting, and then pistols had not been customary.

He saw Charlton advancing with his rifle ready, and he remembered the execution that M. Latour had done with a smaller weapon. So he let fly his first bullet at a distance of thirty or forty yards. It went somewhat wide, and too high. It warned Charlton, and they might have retreated at little risk, but he chose the bolder course. He did not wish to be surrounded in such a position as they then occupied. He ran forward, firing as he did so at the spot from which he thought the bullet had come.

He was not far wrong, and his shots came unpleasantly close to the crouching Demers. No doubt the second pistol was fired the sooner in consequence. Still, there was little wrong with the aim on this occasion.

Charlton felt the bullet strike his right side with such force that he retained his balance with difficulty. It passed on, leaving him with nothing worse than a bruised rib, and some broken skin where it had struck him. He did not know how far he was injured, and he had little leisure to consider it.

He had seen the hand with the levelled pistol, and he fired again at the man whom he knew must be behind it. The shot missed, and the rifle was empty.

He lowered it, and drew out his revolver. He did not know that he had missed, but he wished to make sure.

Then two men ran out of the bushes with cutlasses in their hands, only a few yards away.

He fired at the foremost—fired again—and the man fell. He rolled over, clutching convulsively at the grass. He would give no more trouble. The second hesitated, and ran back. Charlton's shots followed him. He gave a cry of pain as the bushes hid him. He was certainly hit.

The revolver was empty.

So far Demers had not risen. He watched, waiting his chance, while the others risked lives which he felt to be less valuable than his own.

Now he saw Charlton commence to reload the revolver. He knew what that meant, though he had no knowledge of repeating firearms. It was the chance he sought, and he drew his cutlass and came out boldly.

To Charlton it was the supreme test which comes but once or twice in a lifetime. His instinct was to fly. Demers came with a rush, his cutlass lifted over his head. Charlton had the sword slung over his shoulder, which had cumbered him all the day, but he had no skill in its use. Neither in strength was he any match for his brutal enemy.

But Marcelle was behind him, and he could not leave her. He looked for an instant, and saw her, bright-eyed and silent, the child in her arms. She had no doubt what the end would be.

Charlton drew his sword and waited the rush of his opponent. Courage—and ignorance—were his salvation. Demers came with the cutlass raised over his head, meaning that the fight should end with the first blow, as, in fact, it did.

Charlton did not think he could parry such a stroke with success. Probably he was right. It crossed his mind that if he struck straight at Demers' throat he could still kill his enemy even as his own death descended. Marcelle would be saved. Even as the downward stroke was in the air, Demers realised his peril. It was no satisfaction to him to kill Charlton if his own life were to be the price.

Too late, he tried to alter the direction of his stroke, to guard his own throat from the point of which he was running.

In the result, he neither killed Charlton nor saved himself. The cutlass jarred against a blade that was already through his neck, and showed three inches behind it.

Charlton was thrown back against a tree by the force of the rush which he had encountered. His grasp held to the sword-hilt with difficulty as his enemy fell with his weight dragging upon it. He looked down on a face that was convulsed with an insensate fury. Demers struggled on to his hands and knees, and then collapsed again, as his lifeblood pulsed from the wound.

Charlton stepped back quickly as a hairy hand reached out along the turf to grip his foot with no friendly purpose.

But it was the end. Rage fought with death in the glazing eyes, and death conquered.

Marcelle, looking down, said: "Thank you," and then: "Oh, but I am glad that he is dead."

They went on through the dusk.

CHAPTER TWENTY-FIVE

THE TEMPLE

No one followed them further. They looked back at a group that had surrounded their fallen leader, and hurried the faster from the sight, but the pursuit ceased.

Their need was now to reach the temple before the light should fail them.

What reception would wait them there they could not tell, but they went on without discussing its wisdom. Marcelle, at least had no doubt that it was the right thing to do. And they had the child to deliver.

When they reached it, the sun had sunk below the ridge of the western cliffs, and the swift tropic shadows were gathering under the south wall, but they found the steps which the priest had told, and went bravely up them.

They came into a passage which had doorways at intervals. They saw no one. They called, and there was no answer. They hesitated to go further. What right had they there? What explanation could they give if they should be questioned in an alien tongue?

Marcelle set down the child, which had been asleep in her arms. She said "Perhaps she can guide us. Let her go first."

The child went on confidently. She came to the door, or, more accurately, the open archway, which led to the room in which the priest had consulted the mirror. It had no window. It was lighted, as always, by the lamps around it.

There was a heap of rugs in one corner, as there had been previously. Near to these a large leaf, filled with fruit, lay on the floor, with a bowl of water beside it.

The child went straight to these, drank from the bowl, and then commenced eating.

Charlton said: "We must find someone. Will you stay here with the child, while I seek further?"

"No, don't leave me," she answered. "I should be afraid. And besides, can't you see? The food was put here for the child, but it's a man's room. He had her here because there is no one else to take care of her. She tried to follow him because she was frightened to be alone. How she got down those steps—! But you won't find anyone, however long you look. The place is dead."

Charlton wondered if she were right. He looked round at the bare solidity of the chamber—at the shelves of ordered papyri—it all spoke of permanence, and of an established civilisation, however alien from his own.

In some indefinite way it reminded him of the figure in the cave—and of the drawings in the upper chamber, of some of which he would not willingly think—yes, it might even be as old as they. It must have endured very long, and if it were desolate, it could only be a desolation of yesterday. It seemed improbable—and yet her confidence impressed him.

At last he said, "Well, suppose we rest here for tonight, if no one comes to disturb us, and make a search in the morning."

Marcelle agreed, though she knew that such a search would be fruitless; and there was neither night nor day in that unwindowed room where the lamps glowed continually. She rested now.

Charlton looked at the heap of fruit which the child was eating. He was hungry and thirsty. There was enough for all. The child drew back as he approached, with eyes that were shy but not unfriendly. He tried to reassure her with words which could have no meaning to her. She went to Marcelle.

There was a brief silence after that, the child clinging to Marcelle with a hidden face. She was aware of tears, though there was no sound, and her arms tightened to comfort her.

Both she and Charlton were physically exhausted. They were drained of emotion. And their position was difficult. They had become everything to each other, while they were still strangers; it required the interval of sleep to adjust their minds to all its meaning. The presence of the child that had come to them for protection drew them closer, and yet divided them.

But, beyond this, they felt differently.

Marcelle's mind was content and happy. She had won the lover she would have. He had justified her choice, and she had no fear of the future. And, besides, Demers was dead. Life was good; but she was tired now, and would sleep.

She lay down with the child in her arms, and was asleep in an instant; the hardness of a wooden pillow, shaped to the head, which was at one side of the rug-strewn corner, having no power to delay her.

But Charlton could not sleep. He was excited and restless. He paced the chamber continually. He was conscious that he was worn out, and sat down at the table more than once, only to discover that he could not remain still, and to resume his vigil.

So much had happened. So much might still remain to discover—to plan—to avoid. The stake had become so heavy.

He looked down at the sleeping girl, of whom he knew so much, and yet so little.

He had only seen her face a few hours before. He had never more than touched her hand. No—he had once touched her foot in the night, but he did not attempt to repeat it.

She was one of those fortunate girls who look their best when asleep. Fatigue had left her face, where youth triumphed. Her lips smiled, as though a dream had pleased her. Her bare arm was around the child, who slept also, nestling closely, content in its new protection.

The short tunic that she wore did not concern itself to conceal her—and it was torn in places, for the bushes that had met their flight had not all been thornless.

He saw that her body must be sun-brown from heel to head, though only lightly, for which she had to thank the shadowy ways of the forest !eaves.

Only the soles of her dust-stained feet were very dark, polished to a deep chocolate colour by the treading of many boughs.

He looked down at the lithe grace of the sleeping girl, at the smoothly-rounded limbs, and the body that nature had made for motherhood. She moved slightly concealed little. He had an impulse to disturb it further. She was the woman he loved. She was his by her own word. At his life's risk he had won her. Would she thank him in her heart if she woke, and his arms were around her? *"N'oserez vous?"*—yes; but not now. And yet—they might both be dead before another night should know them.

He reached for a rug that lay beside, and drew it over her and the child. He did not know why he did it, or whether it were right, or merely cowardly, or foolish.

He walked up and down the chamber once again, and Marcelle slept the sleep of health and exhaustion, very fortunate in the man she loved.

But still he did not sleep. He sat down again, and laid his head on his arm. He saw the wide-nostrilled face of Demers, with its savage projecting teeth, as it rushed upon him with the lifted cutlass above it. He felt himself borne back as his sword-point took the hairy throat. Vividly he heard Marcelle's voice, he saw her eyes, as she acknowledged his claim upon her in the crowded hall.

He saw many other things which there is no need to detail. He was not used to bloodshed.

Because he could not sleep, he rose again. He looked at the steel mirror that was set into the table. As he gazed, he was aware that it was not steel but water. There were shadows in the water. Steel-blue shadows that moved.

He looked long and closely, and after a time the shadows grew lighter. He saw the houses of the settlement. It was morning. He saw a crowd of men that moved in the direction of the temple. Was he dreaming? he wondered. His eyes left the mirror. He looked at it again and could see clearly that it had a surface of steel. Obviously he had dreamed. Yet he continued to look, and was less sure. It had again an appearance of water. He saw movement again, though this time it was clear almost at once, as though the earlier vision might have commenced in the night-time. This time he saw the sea and the high cliffs as he had first seen them when he had approached the island. Only, he was now looking down from above. He saw a boat—his own boat—come out of the cliff-tunnel. It was full of men, and some women. They were trying to spread the sail. It appeared that they disputed and struggled among themselves as to how this should be done. He saw the overloaded boat heel as the wind caught it.

It was long after that Marcelle woke. Her first sight was of the wide-open eyes of the child, that still lay in the shelter of her arm, and had watched her, silent and unmoving, for many weary hours. Something that was nearly a smile came into the grave eyes, as it knew that she had wakened. It said something which she could not understand. She must teach it her own words.

She kissed it impulsively. It did not draw back, though it had known nothing of the custom of kissing, which was not used by the race from which it came. It reached out a timid hand that touched her face as lightly as a falling leaf. From the ages of separation of race and custom, nature drew them together.

Marcelle rose, yawning. She showed small teeth, white and sharp, that had been taught their use on many nutshells—teeth that she longed to sink in Demers' hand when it came on her shoulder. But that was yesterday. Demers was dead. She looked round, wondering how long she had slept. Charlton was still, his head on his arms. She would not wake him yet. There were physical necessities to consider. She was dirty, and she hated dirt. She must straighten the mass of shortened hair (long hair will catch on the branches—it is too dangerous in the forest) which she had cut and tended as she best knew how for the last two years—but then time was endless. She noticed that the child was busy eating again. There was still some water. But if she used that for washing, where was more to be found? And she was thirsty—and oh! so hungry. Why was the food on the floor? She supposed that the priest had put it there for the child's reaching. It would be a man's way. It confirmed her belief that there had been no one else to take charge of her. It occurred to her that if a child be fed on fruit and water, it is little trouble to anyone. It is the artificial drinks, the composite heated foods, the continual cleansing of solid utensils, which make European life a burden to all who do not control the labour of others, and the rearing of children a weariness to the poor. And they are rewarded for their defiance of Nature with a hundred diseases.

Marcelle did not worry about Nature, or the diet of Europeans. She rarely worried about anything that was more than ten yards away. She merely thought that it is a good way to feed a child to put some fruit on the floor.

As to that, something may depend upon the fruit, something upon the child, something upon the platter selected. There may be other qualifications.

While we have considered the fruit, Marcelle has been busy with other things. She has made herself as tidy as circumstances will permit, and as clean as she can without water. There is a bed-rug which is much the dirtier for her energy. She will not explore the passage alone, though there may be tanks of water at every doorway. Frankly, she is afraid, though she is sure that it is deserted. It is a strange place. Neither will she eat or drink without Charlton. She has decided to wake him.

Stooping over him, she saw the mirror on which his head was pillowed. To her it was a mirror only. But "only" is not a word that she would have used to describe it. It was better even than the forest pool. Marcelle smiled. She looked, and appeared satisfied. She saw a long rent in her shoulder, showing cream-brown flesh, firm and smooth. She did not think it unbecoming. There were lower rents also, which the mirror was unable to show her. She dimpled as she considered them. It is only just to say that she gave another shake to a ragged skirt. But one cannot defend that dimple.

She looked at Charlton with uncompromising Latin eyes that even love would not blind in the seeing. It was an ordeal for any man. He was dishevelled and dirty. So was she, for that matter. She was well content with what she saw, and a song rose to her lips and awakened the silence to unfamiliar melody. He was the man she had chosen, and he had killed Demers to get her. If he had taken her when she slept, she would not have resisted. She had called to him, and he had killed Demers to win her! She was of the nature to pay her debts, even though they were less welcome than this one. But had she known of all that had happened, she would have been glad that he did not. There were many ways in which this game has been played since Adam's rib first ran (but not too fast) from the pursuit of its previous habitation, and of all the ways one is the worst. Life renews itself that its best things may be renewed with it continually, but to each of us they come but once, or twice it may be, and there are few greater follies than to snatch and pass them too hastily.

Seeing that he was still asleep, she bent over him and kissed his neck. He moved instantly, and looked up to see her at the further end of the room, surveying him with a grave demureness. Undeceived by her attitude, his waking mood rose to meet her own. He got up quickly, to feel a sharp pain in his side, that left the eager words upon his lips unspoken.

She was beside him in a moment. "What is it?" she asked anxiously.

He replied: "I think Demers hit me. I hadn't thought of it since. It can't be much." But he was less sure of that than he professed, and the thought that he might have a bullet in his side, with no means of extracting it, was not pleasant.

"Let me look," she said, and they explored together. It was nothing more than a flesh wound that had stiffened and broken out again when he rose so suddenly, and an aching rib that was only bruised, not fractured. But they could not spare any of their remaining water to bathe it. They ate, and drank what was left, and discussed their further action. The presence of the child limited their choice. If they should take it with them, it must impede their progress, either to the caves or the forest. They could not leave it alone. They could not take it without first ascertaining that it had no living parents or others to whom it should be returned. So they decided, though Charlton, at least, saw that either course brought an added danger to a situation which was sufficiently precarious. It seemed to him that it was unreasonable to suppose that the child had no guardians who would be seeking for and must shortly find her. Already they had brought her back from her wandering. To do more was to lose time, and to risk contact with those who were strange and might be hostile. If they could meet with no one, then to take the child would be an encumbrance, and there might be those who would misinterpret it as an outrage, though they were not visible now. It seemed so improbable that they were alone. Even though the temple were deserted, there must surely be life in the buildings that were beyond it.

But it was clear to Marcelle's mind that they could not leave the child. In fact, she did not wish to leave it. By intuition rather than reason, she was sure that they would find no one living. In her own phrase, the place was dead.

To her the search was perfunctory, but she agreed that it must be made. They searched the temple first—the smaller rooms, and then the great hall itself. They saw many strange things, which we need not stop to consider. There may be another time for the telling.

Before they left the chamber in which they slept, Charlton had noticed an open papyrus on which the priest had been writing. Beside it were some books that were amazing, till he thought of the natural explanation. *Pride and Prejudice*, a *Newgate Calendar*, a Bible, a *Nautical Almanac*, the *Speeches of Charles James Fox*, a book on *Farming*, and some others; old and dirty books which the priest had acquired from a generation that had forgotten their use. He saw that the papyrus was partly covered with English words and letters, partly with a writing which seemed unlike anything of which he had knowledge, even of ancient times. He saw that the priest had attempted to probe the mystery of the English books. Possibly in earlier years there may have been those who could help him. Might it be that here was a clue by which the piled wisdom around him could be deciphered, even though its writers had perished?

They searched the remaining chambers in the temple. They went a few paces into the coloured gloom of the temple itself, awful in its desolation. They turned their eyes from the dim figure of Gîr.

They made their way to the buildings behind the temple, finding the sun high in the sky, and learning how long they must have slept as they did so. They searched houses that were silent and desolate, where the dust lay quietly. They saw many strange and some inexplicable things. They found fresh garments which they were glad to take. They found water, and cleansed themselves of the dirt of yesterday.

Charlton was glad to cast aside clothes that were still heavy with the dried slime of the bog, and caked with the blood of Demers (which had spouted over his ankles as the dying wretch had tried to reach him), for the lighter, looser garments that this dead race had worn, and which were cleanly stored in many of the deserted dwellings.

The child walked beside them silently.

They climbed on to a flat roof that gave a wide view, extending to the white walls of the feast-house. The dream or vision of the previous night—Charlton could not decide upon its nature—came back to his mind. He half expected to see that advancing rabble as he had then beheld them.

He saw, instead, a little group that fled across the land with three of the great rukas pursuing them. It was a race that could only have one ending. Running with raised wings, the birds had a speed that would have left a greyhound far behind them. Yet the men panted desperately forward, a race for life of the most literal kind, for there was no hope for the hindmost.

When the birds reached and pulled him down, the others stood still, looking round in bewildered fear, for to run further might be to approach another group of their enemies. Was this all that was left of the visioned crowd that had set out in the morning to seek them while they slept?

They debated whether they should leave the confines of the walls that protected them. Marcelle was anxious to regain the shelter of the forest. She said: "It's not far; I don't think the birds would harm us. I should think they have got all they want by now. Anyway, I think we should be safe from them. Besides, you have the rifle."

Charlton hesitated. He had had enough of fighting, unless it were necessary. But it had to be done. It might really be safer now than later. He answered: "Very well, we'll go at once. If the boat is still safe, we might load up and leave by tomorrow. "

Marcelle was silent. She loved the forest life. She thought that the dangers of the island were over. She had won the mate she needed. She dreaded the thought of the open boat. But that could wait. She only said: "We will go quickly. You will need your hands free for the rifle." She picked up the child.

CHAPTER TWENTY-SIX

A VOICE IN THE NIGHT

They regained the forest without adventure. They noticed that the satyrs were running about in a wild excitement, but they did not molest them.

They crossed the bog and climbed the cliff, finding the opening to the caves without difficulty. The interior was vacant and undisturbed.

It seemed that the adventure of the land was over, and the adventure of the sea was all that lay between them and the civilisation that had been, four days before—to Marcelle at least—a thing remote and unattainable.

Charlton proposed that he should go forward alone to ascertain that the boat and stores were unmolested, while Marcelle waited with the child. Then he would return, and they would rest till morning, and then load the boat and set sail at once, or as soon as the wind were favourable.

But Marcelle would not agree. She would not be separated. She would go with him, even though it meant that they must carry the child. She was silent and irritable. Charlton looked at her with a puzzled wonder. They had come through a great peril together, during which she had been brave and cheerful. They were united not only by a spoken word, but by the sacraments of common loyalties and of common dangers. Yet now that it appeared that they had come through them in triumph, she had become strange and distant. She insisted that he should not leave her, yet she was aloof and silent. She did not meet his eyes, and his words were left unanswered.

Was it strange that he begun to wonder whether she had only used him to assist her extremity, and was now fretting against a bondage that irked her?

For herself, she did not know the meaning of the mood into which she had fallen. Desires and fears warred within her. They warred with hidden faces, so that she could not tell the one from the other. She was averse from any intimacy with Charlton in that narrow chamber, though she would have delighted to have him woo her in the forest night, to what purpose her mind did not face itself to consider. When they came to the shaft beneath which the boat was moored, and saw it swinging uninjured on the ropes that held it, she had a feeling of sharp distress, and realised that her secret hope had been that some disaster had overtaken it.

Charlton said: "If we begin early in the morning, and only load it with that which we most need, we might be away at midday. I took much longer to clear it, but it will be quicker work to lower the things if you are there to receive them."

He spoke of the seaworthiness of the boat, and of the progress they might hope to make with her help in sailing it. If they steered north they had all the North American coast as their objective, and long before they reached it they would be in a fairway of a thousand ships and would surely be rescued.

She did not answer. He led the way back, carrying the lantern; she had the child, who was now tired and half asleep, and clung to her with a frightened shyness.

When they were halfway along the passage, they came to the one that branched aside, which Charlton had not explored previously.

Here she called to him to stop, saying that it led to the chamber which her father had used, and where there would doubtless be the chest in which his papers were kept. She would like to save these.

Charlton suggested, reasonably, that they might get them when returning to the boat in the morning.

She replied that it was drier than the room that opened into the face of the inner cliff. If they had to spend the night in such a cave, they might as well choose the drier.

This was reasonable also, though the tone in which it was spoken was less so. It appeared to Charlton to imply that to stay within the caverns was an evil for which he was responsible.

To him they had seemed a retreat from many dangers, which they should be thankful to have reached together. Fortunately, he had the gift of silence. He had the gift of sympathy also, and through the pain he felt at an estrangement which seemed so causeless he tried to understand the feelings which underlay it.

Perhaps, he thought, she had slept so long beneath green branches and the open stars that she had become impatient of confining walls. Yet she had lain down happily enough in the temple room. No less, he was partly right, though her trouble went deeper.

He went with her along the passage, and they found the room which she was seeking. The chest was there, and its contents were dry and uninjured.

Charlton said: "If you would rather that we stay here, I will fetch anything that we shall need." He hesitated, and added: "Perhaps you would like to be here with the child, and I can watch at the entrance. You will be quite safe. I will close the top of the shaft over the boat."

She said: "I don't know—I will come with you to get the things. But I don't think I shall like it. There is no air here."

They went back together.

They were nearly at the end of the cross-passage when they heard voices.

With a swift motion he obscured and then extinguished the lantern. But the voices had already passed. They were receding toward the chamber beneath which the boat had been moored—the chamber that contained all his possessions.

He felt Marcelle's hand on his arm. They followed silently. There was no need for words. They knew the voices of the island speech; they knew the forms that were revealed by the torches they carried. They saw that their entrance must have been observed, and that they had been followed as soon as the remaining inhabitants of the island had collected such things as they wished to save.

Terrified by the great birds that had now abandoned their usual occupations to chase and feed upon them, their leaders killed, not knowing what vengeance might be impending for the priest's death, it was not wonderful that they had followed Charlton in the hope of discovering some means of flight from the island.

Charlton counted over thirty, as they collected in the chamber over the shaft, scattering his possessions, and searching till they found the stone that covered the shaft, and removed it.

He stood very near to them in the darkness of the passage. Marcelle's hand was still on his arm. She whispered: "Let us go back and talk." He hesitated, and as he did not answer, her grip became firmer, trying to draw him backward.

Had he been alone he would have walked out at once to claim his property. He regarded them as less than human, and he did not think them formidable now that their leaders had fallen.

They should go back the way they came!

But it might be better to do this when he had seen Marcelle and the child in a place of safety. What did these people know about boats? It would be long enough before they had all clambered down the shaft with their lanterns, even should they decide to attempt it. Still, there was no time to lose.

He went back, therefore, at the urging of her hand, feeling the way for a short distance, and then lighting the lantern. He did not care much if they saw it.

They went all the way back, though he became increasingly impatient as they did so. He recognised that, having started, he could not leave her with the child alone in the tunnel darkness.

The sun was near setting. It shone into the aperture, from the sides of which the creepers had now been completely tom by those who had climbed through it, making a transient brilliance in the grey gloom of the chamber, and reflecting itself in the water that dripped in the inner corner.

Marcelle laid down the child, now sleeping soundly, on the bed which Charlton had made on the drier side of the room. Strong though her arm might be, she was glad to be relieved of the burden, but she showed no sign of fatigue when she rose and faced Charlton in the sunlight.

There was a great relief in her heart, and a gay light in her eyes, that surprised him into a momentary forgetfulness of his own impatience. Here again was the spirit that had been so swift in mockery of the thwarted satyr, that had made light of danger as they had run together on the previous night. It was more than that. He felt that the shadow which had fallen between them had cleared away. Here was the Marcelle whom he had known in the night—who had won his love before he had seen her face in the daylight, who had owned him before the table of their enemies, but who was still the girl who had not come to his arms, the stranger whom he had not kissed.

Yet he knew that he must not linger. "You will be safe here," he began, "While...."

She interrupted, as though she did not hear him.

"I suppose they will take the boat," she remarked, as though it were a natural thing, and of little moment that they should do so. A smile parted her lips.

As she said it, she was aware Charlton's arm was around her. "You are divine," he said, and she found herself held close and her head bent back for his kisses.

Then her words penetrated to his mind, and recalled him to the need of the moment. He loosed her reluctantly as he answered.

"No, they mustn't do that. I don't know whether we ought not to try to take them. But they are too many anyway. They might crowd in, of course. But they would overload the boat. It wouldn't be safe, and we couldn't take enough provisions for the risk of a long voyage. No—it wouldn't do."

Then he added doubtfully: "We might take one or two to help with the boat." He had a feeling that there might be some decent ones among them, and that if they wanted to escape he ought to do what he reasonably could.

"I shouldn't come," she answered with a quiet demureness. "But that doesn't matter. I shall be quite happy here."

"You wouldn't—" he began incredulously. "As though I should go without you!"

Her eyes lifted and challenged him, and again his arms were around her. For a moment only she returned his kisses. Then she struggled for freedom. "No," she said, "not here—not here. Did you think I would go with those wretches?" she asked, in the tone of one who is investigating a curiosity of natural history.

"Well, I don't want them," he replied, with an obvious sincerity, "but while we talk they may be capsizing the boat, if they don't get off with it entirely." (How she wished they might!) "If you will stay here, I will soon deal with them."

He turned to go, but with a quick movement she was between him and the passage.

"What do you mean to do?" she asked quietly.

"I shall send them the way them came," he answered. "The goods are mine, and so is the boat. I don't think they will be much trouble."

She did not move. "You forget," she said, "that they will have found the arms you left there."

That was true. He had forgotten. He had only told her casually of them in the long talk of their night in the forest. He was surprised that she remembered. There were arms there more formidable than their clumsy muskets. But they might not easily find out how to use them.

"I don't think that will make any difference," he answered stubbornly. "If you want the boat clear, you shall have it."

She broke out with a sudden change of mood, when she realised how hard it was to deflect his purpose. "Do you care nothing that you will leave me here alone? Do you think that nothing can kill you? *You will tempt God too far!*"

He was surprised at her vehemence, which seemed unreasonable.

"But what else can we—?" he began, and was interrupted.

"Cannot you see that we are safer here? There is no danger left, unless you make it. Why should we drown in a boat? *It is all ours, if you will let them go.*"

Then her tone changed as she stepped aside to let him go if he would. "Of course, you can do as you like," she said pleasantly. "Some people like caves and boats. I like the forest."

She gave an instant's glance at the child, who was sleeping soundly. She looked at Charlton again with mocking eyes. "Bogs," she remarked, "are best crossed in the daylight."

The sun, that was now only half visible above the cliffs of the western side of the island, caught the darkness of his hair as she turned and slipped out of the opening.

Charlton, following, saw her dropping down the creepers at a speed that he could hardly hope to equal.

He followed her through the failing light, but he got no nearer. He followed till her form became dim in the growing gloom, though she fled no faster than he pursued her. At last he followed only a voice that called and mocked him.

"N'oserez vous?
N'oserez vous?
N'oserez vous, mon bel ami?"

Now it was the night in the forest.
He followed a voice in the night.

ABOUT THE AUTHOR

SYDNEY FOWLER WRIGHT (1874-1965) penned over seventy volumes of science fiction, fantasy, classic mysteries, historical novels, poetry, and non-fiction, many of them being published by the Borgo Press Imprint of Wildside Press.

www.ingramcontent.com/pod-product-compliance
Lightning Source LLC
Chambersburg PA
CBHW031431250626
47155CB00004B/1697